D0806182

THE BRIDAL MARCH,
AND OTHER STORIES.

"On the way out of church Hans paused in front of the church door." — Page 110.

THE BRIDAL MARCH, AND OTHER STORIES.

BY

BJÖRNSTJERNE BJÖRNSON.

TRANSLATED FROM THE NORSE

BY

RASMUS B. ANDERSON

Short Story Index Reprint Series

BOOKS FOR LIBRARIES PRESS
FREEPORT, NEW YORK

First Published 1882

Reprinted 1969

STANDARD BOOK NUMBER:

8369-3136-X

LIBRARY OF CONGRESS CATALOG CARD NUMBER:

74-98562

PRINTED IN THE UNITED STATES OF AMERICA

PREFACE.

"The Bridal March" (Brudeslaatten) was published in 1872, and was dedicated to Hans Christian Andersen, the celebrated Danish story-teller. This is the last of the author's peasant novels, and he will probably never produce another. He has become more and more deeply interested in the great social and political questions of the century, and the stories and dramas he now writes are imbued with the progressive spirit of the age.

The four striking illustrations in this volume were made expressly for "The Bridal March" by Norway's most distinguished *genre* painter, Adolf Tidemand, who was born in 1814 and died in 1876. He made a specialty of illustrating the character, customs, and manners of Norwegian country life, and in this field of art he has never been equaled by any other Scandinavian painter. His delineation of faces, interiors, the every-day life, and the solemnities and festivities of the Norwegian peasantry, secured him the admiration of the world, and are as faithful to reality as one of Björnson's peasant stories. I doubt not that the four illustrations by Tidemand in this volume will be studied with as much pleasure as the story itself.

Eight of Björnson's short stories will be found in this volume: "Thrond," written in 1856; "A Dangerous Wooing," in 1856; "The Bear Hunt," in 1857; "The Father," in 1858; "The Eagle's Nest," in 1859; "Blakken," in 1868; "Fidelity," in 1868; and "A Problem of Life," in 1869. The rest of the author's short stories, including "Dust," written in 1882, will appear in the next volume.

"Captain Mansana," the next story in this series, will illustrate Björnson's skill in dealing with modern life in Italy.

RASMUS B. ANDERSON.

ASGARD, MADISON, WISCONSIN,
May, 1882.

CONTENTS.

THE BRIDAL MARCH.

THERE dwelt in one of the larger mountain valleys of Norway, some time during the last century, a fiddler, whose name after him passed, in a measure, into legendary lore. Quite an array of songs and dances are ascribed to him; some of these, according to tradition, he learned from the underground folk, one from the Evil One himself, one he made for the purpose of saving his life, etc. One of his tunes has become famous beyond all the others, for its history did not end with his life, it really began after he was dead.

The fiddler, Ole Haugen, a poor houseman living far up the mountain, had a daughter named Aslaug, who had inherited his fine head and his musical talent, if not for playing at least for everything else of the same nature; for she was easy and self-possessed in conversation, in singing, in her walk, and in dancing; and had, too, a very flexible voice, a common thing in her family. The third son of the ancient house of Tingvold, a young man, returned from distant lands. His two brothers, both of them older than he, had been drowned in a freshet, and he was now heir to the gard. He met Aslaug at a large wedding-party and fell in love with her. It was an unheard-of thing in those days for a gardman's son of so old and prominent a family to woo one in Aslaug's circumstances and rank of life. This young man, however, had been long absent from home, and he gave his parents to understand that he had ample means abroad for his support ; if he could not have what he wanted at home, he said, it mattered little to him what became of the gard. It was universally prophesied that such disregard of his family and the inheritance of his forefathers, would bring its own punishment ; it was said, too, that Ole Haugen must have influenced him, and perhaps with help that every mortal should fear.

While the struggle between the young man and his parents was going on, Ole Haugen, so it is stated, had been in the most excellent spirits. But when the victory was won, he is said to have announced that he had already made a bridal march for the young couple ; it could never by any possibility be lost to the

"Randi . . . sat with her daughter's little child in her lap." — Page 11.

house of Tingvold; but Heaven have mercy on the bride, he is furthermore charged with having said, who did not drive to church to its strains with as happy a heart as that of the houseman's daughter from Haugen! And this led people to suspect some evil influence

This is the tradition, and it is like so many others. But something more reliable than tradition is the fact, that in this as well as in other mountain parishes there exists, even to the present day, a lively taste for music and ballads, and in past times it must have been still keener. Such tastes can only be preserved through those who are able to enlarge and embellish the inherited treasure-stores, and Ole Haugen certainly possessed this power to a remarkable degree.

Tradition states, furthermore, that as Ole Haugen's bridal march was the most joyous one that had ever been heard, so the first bride and groom that drove home to its music, after having been conducted by the same to the church door, and met there again by the glad sounds at the conclusion of the ceremony, were the happiest couple that had ever been seen. And although the Tingvold family had always been a handsome race, and after this time became still more noted for its beauty, yet legendary lore stoutly asserts that this bridal pair must carry off the palm through all coming generations.

We pass now from tradition to firmer ground; for with Ole Haugen legendary lore dies; after him history begins. The latter tells us that this bridal march became an heir-loom in the family, differing from other heir-looms, which seldom are of any use; for this *was used*, that is to say, the tune was sung, shouted, whistled, tooted, played from house to stable, from the home-fields to the woodland pasture; and to its glad strains the only child the couple ever had was rocked and dandled in the arms of its mother, its father, the nurse-maid, and the rest of the household servants; and the first thing it learned after its earliest tricks and words was the bridal march. The child was called Astrid. There was music in the family, and particularly in this sprightly little girl, who could soon sing with a tra-la-la, in a masterly way, the bridal march, the victory shout of her parents, the promise of her family. It was, indeed, no wonder that when she was grown up she insisted upon making her own choice of a lover. Perhaps rumor has exaggerated the number of Astrid's suitors; but one thing is certain: this wealthy girl, with her refined nature, when over twenty-three years of age, was not yet betrothed. Then at last the cause of this came to light! Several years before her mother had taken in from the highway a bright gypsy lad; he was not really a gypsy lad, but was called so, and especially by Astrid's mother when it reached her ears that her daughter and he had most strangely entered into a betrothal up in the woodland pasture, and that now they passed their time in singing the bridal march to each other, she from the store-house roof, he from the slope above. The youth was quickly sent away; for now it appeared that no one held more strictly to the "family" than the former houseman's daughter. And the father could not help thinking of the prophecy made when he himself violated the customs of his family. They of the house of Tingvold were already giving their children in marriage to people from the highway. Where would this end? The parish did not judge more leniently. The gypsy lad — Knut was his name — had taken to trading, especially in cattle, and was known to every one. He was the first person in this parish, indeed for miles round, who had gone into the business on so large a scale. He opened this avenue of trade, and thus procured for the parishes better prices for their stock, and increased the wealth of many a family. But this did not prevent carousing and fighting from following in his footsteps wherever he went, and this was the only thing that people talked about; for his worth as a trader they did not yet understand. By the time Astrid was twenty-three years old, it had become pretty evident that either the gard must pass out of the direct line of descent, or this man would have to be taken into it; for Astrid's parents had, through their own marriage, lost the moral power which might have enabled them to take compulsory measures. So Astrid had her way: the lively, handsome Knut drove to church with her one fine day, at the head of an immense procession. The bridal march of the house of Tingvold, the grandfather's masterpiece, flashed back over the train of followers, and the young couple sat as though they were joining in the merry tune with a low tra-la-la, for they looked very blithe and gay. People were astonished to see that the parents also seemed in good spirits; they had made such long and persevering resistance.

After the wedding, Knut undertook the management of the farm, and the old people had a yearly allowance made them; but this was so large that no one could understand how Knut and Astrid were able to afford it; for although the gard was the largest in the parish, it was far from being in a good condition. Nor was this all; the working force was increased threefold, and new methods were introduced at an expense hitherto unheard of in that region. Certain ruin was predicted for him. But the "gypsy lad," as Knut was still called, maintained his cheerfulness, and his high spirits infected Astrid. The delicate, shy maiden of yore had become a stirring, robust housewife. Her parents were consoled. At last people began to find out that Knut had brought to Tingvold what no one had had there before: *capital for carrying on the farming!* He had, moreover, brought large experience from his rambling life, besides a faculty for handling merchandise and money, and for keeping laborers and servants good-natured and cheerful; and so at the end of twelve years Tingvold could scarcely have been recognized. The houses were entirely changed, the farm stock was increased threefold, and was three times better kept than before, and Knut himself in a dress-coat, with a "meerschaum pipe," and a glass of toddy, passed his evenings with the captain, the priest, and the lensmand. Astrid adored him as the wisest and best man on earth;

and she herself told that in his youth he now and then got into fights and drank too much, simply that rumors of his doings might reach her ears and alarm her; "for he was such a shrewd fellow." She followed his example in everything, except in making a change in her dress and habits; she preferred keeping to the peasant customs and dress. Knut always allowed others to follow their own inclinations; and so no discord entered his home because of Astrid's wishes. He lived his own way and she waited on him. It was a frugal life he led, be it observed; he was too sensible to care to make a great noise or to incur heavy expense. Some said that he made at card-playing, and through the importance and associations it opened to him, *more* than it cost him to live; but this was doubtless mere scandal.

They had several children, whose history does not concern us; but the eldest son, Endrid, who was to succeed to the gard, was also expected to increase its honors. He was handsome, like all the rest of his family; but his mind was only adapted to common-place affairs, as may often be observed in the children of enterprising parents. His father early noticed this, and resolved to supply the boy's deficiencies through a superior education. For this reason the children had a private tutor; and Endrid, when grown, was sent to one of the agricultural schools, which at this time were just being improved, and later to the city. He came home again a quiet boy, who showed marks of overstudy, and who had fewer city habits than could have been anticipated, or than his father desired. Endrid was, in fact, by no means quick at learning.

Numerous were the speculations made on this boy, both by the captain and the priest, each of whom had several daughters; but if this were the cause of the increased consideration they showed Knut, they deceived themselves very badly indeed, for Knut so thoroughly despised a marriage with a poor captain's or priest's daughter, who was without preparation for the management of the affairs of a large gard, that he did not even deem it worth his while to warn his son. Nor was it needful that he should: the young man saw as clearly as he that the family required something more than merely being raised to prosperity, and that it must now mingle with the blood of those who were its equals in age and respectability. But the misfortune was that the youth was somewhat awkward when he went on his matrimonial errands, and people mistrusted him.

This might not have made so much difference had he not gained the reputation of being on the lookout for a good match, and peasants are always shy of one of whom such things are said. Endrid himself soon noticed this; for if he was not very shrewd, he was, on the other hand, extremely sensitive. He perceived that it in nowise bettered his situation that he had the clothes and manners of the city, as people said. And as at bottom there was something really worthy in this boy, the effect of his mortification was that he gradually laid aside his city dress and city speech and set to work on his father's immense gard, like any common laborer. His father understood it all; indeed, he knew before the young man understood it himself, and he begged the boy's mother not to appear to notice anything. Therefore they said nothing to their son about marriage, and no further heed was paid to the change which had taken place in him, than that his father, with ever-increasing kindness of manner, admitted him to his plans about the farming and other family concerns, and gradually placed the entire management of the gard in his son's hands. He never had cause to regret having done so.

Thus matters stood with the son until he was thirty-one years old, having increased his father's property and his own experience and prudence. During all this time he had made no attempt, no, not the slightest, to court any of the girls in or out of the parish, and now his parents began to grow seriously uneasy lest he had entirely put marriage out of his head. But this he had not done.

In the neighboring gard there lived, in good circumstances, a family of the best blood in the parish, and one that had several times, too, intermarried with the ancient house of Tingvold. There grew up there a young girl, in whom Endrid had taken an interest from the time she was a little child; very likely he had in secret set his heart on her, for only half a year after her confirmation he offered himself to her. She was seventeen years old, he thirty-one. Randi, that was her name, could not at once make up her mind what answer she should give him; she went to her parents about it, but they told her they would leave it entirely to herself. They thought Endrid was a most worthy man, and that, as far as property went, this was the best match she could make. The difference in age was great, and she must herself decide whether she, young as she was, had the courage to assume the responsibilities of the large gard and the many unfamiliar duties. Randi knew very well that her parents would rather have her say Yes than No; but she was really alarmed. So she went over to see Endrid's mother, whom she had always liked. She took it for granted that his mother knew of his suit, but found to her astonishment that she knew nothing about it. The good mother was so delighted that she used all her powers of persuasion to induce Randi to say Yes.

"I will help you," said she. "Father will not accept any annuity; he has his own means, and he does not want his children to grudge him his life. There will at once be a general division of the property, and the little which we shall hereafter have for our support will then be divided after we are gone. From this you can judge that you will not be taking on yourself any annoyances so far as we are concerned."

Yes, Randi knew very well that Astrid and Knut were kind.

"And our boy," continued Astrid, "is good and considerate."

Yes, Randi had learned that for herself; she was not afraid of getting on with him — if she were only worthy herself.

A few days later the matter was settled, and if Endrid was happy, so too were his parents, for he was about to marry into a highly-esteemed family, and the girl herself was so pretty and so sensible that in those respects there had perhaps never been a better match in the parish. The old people of both families conferred together about the wedding, which was arranged to take place just before harvest, for there was no occasion for waiting in this case.

The parish, meanwhile, did not receive these tidings in the same manner as the parties interested. It was thought that the pretty young girl had "sold herself." She was so young that she could scarcely know what marriage meant, and the wily Knut had no doubt urged his son on before the girl was as yet ready for suitors. A little of this talk reached Randi's ears, but Endrid was so affectionate, and that in such a quiet, almost humble way, that she would not break with him, yet she grew rather cold. The parents of both had no doubt also heard one thing and another, but acted as though all were well.

The marriage was to be celebrated in grand style, perhaps just to defy gossip, and for that same reason the preparations were not displeasing to Randi. Knut's associates, the priest, the captain, and the lensmand, with the whole of their large families, were to accompany the bridal party to church. That was why Knut did not wish any fiddling — it was too old-fashioned and countrified; but Astrid insisted that the bridal march of the family must conduct the young couple to church and thence back home again; they had been too happy with it themselves, she said, not to have the satisfaction of enjoying its repetition on the marriage day of their dear children. Knut did not trouble himself much about poetry and things of that sort; he let his wife settle the matter. A hint was given to the bride's parents, therefore, that the fiddlers might be engaged, and the old march, which had been allowed to rest for a while, because the present representatives of the family worked without song, was requested.

The wedding day unfortunately set in with a furious autumnal rain. The fiddlers were forced to cover up their instruments after having played the party out of the gard, and they did not bring them forth again until they had gone far enough to hear the church-bells ringing. A boy was obliged to stand behind them on the cart holding an umbrella over them, and beneath it they sat huddled together, scraping away. The march did not sound well in such weather, as might be expected, neither did the bridal party that followed look happy. The bridegroom had his wedding hat tucked away between his knees, and a southwester on his head; he had a large leathern jacket drawn over his shoulders, and he held an umbrella over the bride, who had kerchief upon kerchief wrapped about her to protect her crown and the rest of her finery, and who had rather the appearance of a hay-mow than a human being. Thus they drove on, cart after cart, the men dripping, the women bundled up and concealed from view; it was a mysterious sort of a bridal party, in which not a face could be seen or recognized, only a quantity of rolled up heaps of wool or fur stowed closely together. The unusually great throng that had gathered along the road-side to see the wealthy bridal party pass by had to laugh, at first in suppressed tones, but finally louder and louder, as each cart passed. Near the large house where the party had to alight to arrange their dress before entering the church, a peddler, a droll fellow, whose name was Aslak, was standing on a hay-cart which had driven out of the way into the corner by the shed. Just as the bride was being lifted out of the cart, he shouted, —

"The deuce a bit will Ole Haugen's bridal march sound to-day!"

A laugh arose in the crowd, and the almost universal effort to suppress this only made it the more apparent what every one thought and was striving to conceal.

When the kerchiefs were removed from the bride, they saw that she was as white as a sheet. She wept, tried to laugh, then wept again, and then all at once she took it into her head that she would not go to church! Amid the commotion that now followed, she had to be laid down on a bed in a side-room, for she was seized with a fit of weeping that alarmed every one. Her worthy parents stood by, and when she implored them to spare her from going into church, they said that she must do as she pleased. Then her eyes sought Endrid. Any one so unhappy, aye, so utterly helpless, she had never seen, for to him there had been truth in their compact. At his side stood his mother; she said nothing and not a muscle of her face moved. But tear after tear trickled down her cheeks; her eyes hung on Randi's. At last Randi raised herself up on her elbows, stared for a while right before her, sobbing through her tears, and presently she said, —

"Oh yes! I will go to church."

Then flinging herself back on the pillow again, she wept for a time, bitterly; but after this she rose. Later she added, that she did not want any more music, and she was allowed to have her way. But the dismissed fiddlers did not improve the story when they mingled with the crowd outside.

It was a sorry bridal procession which now moved toward the church. The rain, of course, permitted the bride and bridegroom to hide their faces from the curiosity of the multitude until they entered the church; but they felt that they were running the gauntlet and that their own large company were ill pleased at having been deluded into taking part in such a fool's errand.

The famous fiddler, Ole Haugen, was buried close by the church door. By common consent his grave had been protected: one of his family had placed a new head-board there, as the old one had decayed around the bottom. The head-board was shaped like a wheel at the top, Ole himself had left orders to have it so. The grave was on a sunny spot, and countless wild flowers grew there. Every church-goer that had ever stood by this grave, knew, from one source or another, that a man who at state expense had been collecting plants and flowers in the surrounding villages and mountains, had found flowers on this grave which did not grow for miles around. The effect was, that the peasants who usually cared little for what they called "weeds," felt an inquisitive delight in these flowers, perhaps too, an inquisitive shyness; some of the flowers were uncommonly pretty. Now as the bridal pair walked past this grave, Endrid, who held Randi by the hand, noticed that a shudder ran through her; for it seemed to her that Ole Haugen's ghost had been walking to-day. Immediately afterward her tears began to flow again, consequently she entered the church weeping, and was led weeping to her seat. Thus no bride had been known to come into this church in the memory of man.

Randi felt, as she sat there, that she was now confirming the rumor that was afloat about her having been sold. The terrible disgrace to her parents that there was in this, caused her to grow cold and for a while to be able to restrain her tears. But at the altar she became agitated again over some remark or other of the priest, and at once all that she had experienced this day rushed upon her; it seemed to her for a time as though she could never look people in the eyes again, least of all her parents.

All the rest is but a repetition of what we have been over, and therefore there is nothing further to report except that she could not sit down to dinner with the company, and when entreaties and threats brought her to the supper-table she spoiled all pleasure there and had to be taken to bed. The wedding party that was to have lasted several days, broke up that same evening. "The bride was ill," it was announced.

Although no one believed this, it was, nevertheless, but too true. Randi was no longer well, nor was she ever very hearty again. And one of the results was that the first child of this couple was sickly. The love of the parents for this little one was naturally none the less devoted, because they both understood that they were, in a certain way, responsible for its suffering. They associated with no one except this child; to church they never went; they were afraid of people. For two years God granted them their happiness with their child, and then He took this too.

The first clear thought they could command after this blow was that they had been too fond of the child. That was why they had lost it. And so when another child was born unto them, it seemed as if neither of them dared bestow much affection on it. But the child, who in the beginning appeared as sickly as the first, revived, and became much more sprightly than the other had been, so that its charms were irresistible. A new, pure joy entered their hearts; they could forget what had befallen them when they were with their child. When the little one was two years old, God took it also.

There are some people who are singled out by sorrow. They are just the very ones who seem to us *least* to need it, but they are, nevertheless, best fitted to bear testimony of faith and self-denial. This couple had early sought God together; henceforth their sole communion was with Him. There had long been a hush over life at Tingvold, now it became like a church before the priest enters. Work went on undisturbed, but between every hour of labor Endrid and Randi had a little time of devotion, in which they communed with those on the other side. It caused no change when, shortly after the last loss, Randi gave birth to a daughter; the two children who had died were sons, and a girl was for this reason hardly acceptable to the parents. Moreover, they knew not if she would be spared to them. But the health and happiness the mother had enjoyed just before the loss of the last boy had been of advantage to the child she was then expecting; it early proved to be an unusually lively little girl, with the mother's fair face in the bud. The temptation again came over these two lonely people to cling to their child with hope and joy; but the fateful two years had not yet come, and when it did arrive, it seemed to them as if they had merely gained a respite. They dared not yield to their feelings.

The two old people had held themselves much aloof. For the mood that controlled the others could be approached neither with words of consolation nor with the joys of others. Knut was, moreover, too fond of worldly pleasure to remain long in a house of mourning or to be forever taking part in devotional exercises. So he moved over to a small farm which he owned, and which he hitherto had rented; now he took it himself and put it in such fine, tasteful order for his dear Astrid that she, who would greatly have preferred being at Tingvold, remained where *he* was, and laughed with him instead of weeping with their children.

One day when Astrid went over to visit her daughter-in-law, she saw little Mildred, and she observed that the child was left entirely to herself; the mother scarcely ventured to touch her. Moreover, the grandmother noticed that when the father came in, he manifested the same sorrowful reserve toward his only child. Astrid concealed her thoughts, but when she got home to her own dear Knut, she represented to him what a wretched state of affairs there was at Tingvold; *there* was now their place. Little Mildred ought to have some one who was not afraid to take pleasure in her; for there was growing up something very fine and fair for the family in this child. Knut was impressed by his wife's eager zeal, and both the old people packed up and went home.

Mildred thus became the special care of the grandparents, and the old people taught the parents to love the child. But when Mildred was five years old there was born to the house another daughter, who was named Beret, and the result was that Mildred passed most of her time with the old people.

Now the frightened parents once more began to dare believe in life! To this the change in the atmosphere about them contributed not a little. After the loss of the second child people always noticed that they had wept, but never saw them in tears; their sorrow was very unobtrusive.

The peaceful, pious life at Tingvold, bound the servants to the place; and many words of praise of the master and mistress were spoken abroad. They became sensible of this themselves. Both relatives and friends began to seek them out and continued to do so, even though the Tingvold family made no return.

But at church they had not been since their wedding-day. They partook of the sacrament at home, and conducted their own devotional services. But when the second girl was born they felt a desire to be her sponsors themselves, so for the first time they ventured to church. Upon this occasion they visited together the graves of their children, and they walked past Ole Haugen's resting-place without a word or a gesture, and all the people showed them respect. Nevertheless, they continued to live to themselves, and a pious hush lay over the whole gard.

Here one day, at her grandmother's house, little Mildred sang the bridal march. In great alarm old Astrid stopped her work and asked the child where in all the world she had learned this tune. Mildred replied that she had learned it of her.

Old Knut who was sitting there had a good laugh at this, for he knew very well that Astrid had a habit of humming it when she had any work that kept her sitting still. But now little Mildred was begged by both grandparents not to sing the tune when her parents could hear. A child is very apt to ask "why?" But when Mildred did so, she received no reply. After this the little girl heard the new herd-boy singing the tune one evening while he was chopping wood. She told this to her grandmother who had also heard it; but Astrid only remarked: "Ah, he will never grow old here!" and sure enough, the next day the boy was sent away. There was no reason given him; he simply was paid his wages and dismissed. Now Mildred became so excited that her grandmother had to endeavor to tell her the history of the bridal march. The little eight-years old girl understood it pretty well, and what she did not understand then became clear to her later. The story exercised on her childhood an influence which nothing else ever did or could produce: it laid the foundation for her future relations to her parents.

Children have an astonishingly early perception of and sympathy for those who are unhappy. Mildred felt that in the presence of her parents all should be still. This was not difficult to put into practice; for they were so gentle and talked to her so incessantly about the kind heavenly Friend of little children, that the room glowed with a magic light. But the story of the bridal march gave her a touching comprehension of what they had passed through. Painful memories she carefully avoided, and manifested a heartfelt affection in all that she dared share with them, and this was their piety, their truthfulness, their quiet ways, their industry. As Beret grew up, she gradually learned to do the same; for woman's vocation as an educator is awakened from childhood up.

In the society of the grandparents the spirits that in the family home were under restraint flowed freely. Here there was singing and dancing; games were played and nursery tales told. And thus the sisters, as they were growing up, divided their time between deep devotion to their melancholy parents in the quiet family sitting-room, and the merry life in the home of their grandparents; but it was so gently divided that it was their parents who besought them to go enjoy themselves with the old people; and the old people who entreated them go back to their parents and "be right good girls."

When a girl of from twelve to sixteen years of age takes into her full confidence a sister of from seven to eleven, she gains as a reward an unbounded devotion. But the younger one is apt to become a little too matured thereby.

Mildred herself, on the other hand, was the gainer in becoming forbearing, compassionate, sympathetic, affable, and she became a source of silent joy to both parents and grandparents.

There is nothing further to narrate until Mildred entered her fifteenth year; then old Knut died, suddenly and easily. Scarcely a moment passed from the time he sat jesting in his home until he lay there a corpse.

The pleasantest thing the grandmother knew after his death was to have Mildred on the little cricket at her feet, where she had been in the habit of having her sit from the time Mildred was small, and either herself to tell the child about Knut, or to have Mildred sing, with a low tra-la-la, the bridal march. In *its* tones Astrid saw Knut's vigorous, dark head emerge from her childhood; in listening to it she could follow him over the grassy slopes of the gard, where as a herd-boy he used to blow his horn; in it she drove to church at his side; in it his merry, clever image most distinctly rose up before her. But in Mildred's soul there began to stir new emotions. While she sat singing to her grandmother, she asked herself: "Will this bridal march ever be played for me?"

From the moment this question presented itself to her, it grew; the march became all aglow with a calm, peaceful happiness. She saw a bridal crown glittering in its sunshine, which opened out a long, bright future for her to ride forward in. She reached the age of sixteen, and she asked herself: "Shall I — ah! shall I ever drive after it myself, followed by father and mother, past a crowd of people who do not laugh, alight with a joyous heart where mother wept, walk past Ole Haugen's grave, and up to the altar in such radiant bliss that father and mother shall have amends for all that they have suffered?"

This was the first train of thought she did not confide to Beret. As time wore on there came to be others. Beret, who was now in her twelfth year, saw plainly that she was left more to herself than she had been, but did not exactly understand that she was being set aside until another was in possession of her privileges. This was the eighteen-years-old, just betrothed, Inga, their cousin who lived on the neighboring gard. When Beret saw her and Mildred go whispering and laughing across the fields, with their arms entwined about each other, after the wont of young girls, she was ready to fling herself down and weep with jealousy.

Mildred was now preparing for confirmation;

thus she became acquainted with those of her own age, and some of them came on Sundays up to Tingvold. They spent their time out in the fields, or in grandmother's house. Tingvold had indeed hitherto been a closed land of promise to the young people of the parish. Nor did there now come any but those of a certain gentle, quiet nature, for it could not be denied that there was something subdued about Mildred that attracted but few.

In those days there was a great deal of singing going on among the young people. Such things are never accidental; nevertheless they have their seasons, and these seasons again have their leaders. Among the latter, oddly enough, there was once more a member of the Haugen family. Wherever there can be found a people, among whom, however many hundred years past it may have been, almost every man and woman have sought and found in song an expression for their deepest feelings and thoughts, and have been themselves able to make the verses which bore the outpourings of their souls, — there the art can never so entirely die out but that it may still live at some parish merry-making, and can easily be awakened even where it has not been heard for a long time. In this parish there had been made many verses, and much music from time out of mind; it was neither *from* nothing nor *for* nothing that Ole Haugen was born here. And now it was his son's son in whom the musical taste of the family lived. Ole Haugen's son had been so much younger than the daughter who had married into the Tingvold family, that she as a married woman had stood sponsor for him. After many changes of fortune, he had, when quite an old man, become proprietor of his father's freeholder's place up the mountain, and singularly enough he had then married for the first time. Several children were born to him, and among them a son, who was called Hans, and who seemed to have inherited his grandfather's talents, not exactly for fiddling, although he did play, but rather for singing old songs and sometimes composing new ones. His taste for music was largely increased through his knowing so few people, although he lived right in their midst. Moreover, there were, indeed, not many who had seen him. The fact was, his old father had been a huntsman, and before his sons were very large the old man used to sit on the hill-side and teach them to load and take aim. His delight is said to have been exceedingly great when the little fellows could earn the powder and shot they used.

Beyond this he never got. Their mother died a short time after him, so the children were left to take care of themselves, and they did so. The boys went hunting, and the girls managed the place on the mountain. They attracted attention when, once in a while, they made their appearance in the valley, but this was not often, for in the winter there was no path, and they had to be content with the trips about the surrounding neighborhood which must be made to sell and carry to its destination their game; and in the summer they were kept in the mountains with travelers. Their place was the highest one in the parish; it was celebrated for having that pure mountain air which is more successful in healing lung weaknesses and shattered nerves than any known medicine, and so every year it was overrun with people from town or from abroad. The family added several buildings to their place; but still their rooms were filled. From poor, aye, pitiably poor people, these brothers and sisters had thus worked their way up to prosperity. Intercourse with so many strangers had given them a peculiar stamp; they had even learned something of the foreign languages. Several years before Hans had bought the place of his brothers and sisters, so that it stood in his name; he was at this time twenty-eight years old.

None of them had ever set foot in the home of their Tingvold relatives. Endrid and Randi Tingvold had certainly not consciously forbidden this; but they could tolerate the mention of the name Haugen as little as they could the sound of the bridal march. The poor father of these children had upon one occasion been made to feel this, and so Hans forbade his brothers and sisters to go there. But the Tingvold girls, who took so much pleasure in singing, had an incredible desire to know Hans, and felt ashamed that their parents had neglected these relatives. In the recent gatherings of girls at the gard, there were more questions asked and more anecdotes told about Hans and his brothers and sisters than about anything else.

In the midst of this delightful period of song and social intercourse, Mildred was confirmed, at the approach of her seventeenth year. A little while before this all had been quiet about her; a short time after it was the same. But in the spring, or rather in the summer, she was to go up to the sæter with the cattle, as all girls do after they are confirmed. She was exceedingly glad! Her betrothed friend Inga was to be at the neighboring sæter.

Beret was to be allowed to accompany her

sister to the sæter, and Mildred's longing affected her also. But when they got up to the sæter, where Beret became completely absorbed in all the unaccustomed surroundings, Mildred continued to be as restless as before; she went about her work with the cattle and the dairy in an absent-minded manner; but the long weary time that still remained hung heavily on her hands. For hours together she would sit with Inga, listening while she talked of her lover, then would not go near her for days. If Inga came to see her, she was pleased and affectionate, and acted as though she repented her faithlessness, but she soon grew tired of her again. She seldom had anything to say to Beret, and often when Beret addressed her the child got no other answers than Yes and No. Beret went weeping after the cattle and joined the herd-boys. Mildred felt that there was something in all this that had been broken to pieces; but with the best will she knew not how to mend it.

With such thoughts as these, she was one day sitting in the vicinity of the sæter green. Some goats had found their opportunity to straggle away from the flock, and she had to watch them. It was in the forenoon of a warm day; she sat in the shade of a ridge overgrown with young trees and birch; she had thrown off

"There she comes," thought she, and looked up." — Page 41

her jacket and taken out her knitting. She was expecting Inga. She heard a rustling behind her. "There she comes," thought she, and looked up.

But a louder noise followed than it seemed to her Inga could make; the bushes crackled and creaked under a heavy tread; Mildred grew pale and started up, and saw a rim of fur and a pair of blinking eyes underneath; it must be a bear's head! She felt a desire to scream, but could not find voice; she wanted to spring up, but could not stir. Then the object that had startled her was drawn up full length before her; it proved to be a tall, broad-shouldered man, with a fur cap and a gun in his hand. He paused suddenly among the young trees and looked at her. His eyes were keen, but in constant motion; he made a few steps forward, then with a bound stood on the greensward at her side. Something brushed against her knee; she gave a low scream. It was his dog, whom she had not seen before.

"Ugh!" cried she. "I almost thought it was a bear that was trampling down the young trees, that is the reason why I was so frightened."

She tried to laugh.

"Ah, you were not far from the truth!" said

he, and he spoke with extraordinary gentleness. "Kvas and I were just on the track of a bear, but we have lost it; and if there be any wraith[1] accompanying *me*, it is certainly a bear."

He smiled. She stared at him. What sort of a person was this? Tall, broad-shouldered, with eyes that were constantly changing, so that she could not look into them; and thus he stood close beside her as if he had sprung out of the earth, with his gun and his dog. She felt a strong impulse to say: "Go away from me!" but instead she herself drew back a few paces, and asked: "Who are you?" for she was actually afraid.

"Hans Haugen," he replied absently; for his attention had been called to the dog, that had evidently found the scent again. He turned hastily toward her to say farewell; but when he looked at her he saw the young girl standing before him, with the hot blood gushing up in streams over cheeks, neck, and throat.

"What is the matter!" cried he, astonished.

She knew not what to do, whether she should run away, turn round, or sit down.

"Who are you? asked he.

At once she was again bathed in blushes;

[1] The old superstition, that every man has his wraith (vardöger) in his train (an invisible animal, which is an expression of his nature), is still common among the peasants. — TRANSLATOR.

for to tell him her name would be to explain all she had in thought in regard to him.

"*Who are you?*" he asked once more,—which was the most natural question in the world, and certainly deserved an answer; nor could she refuse one; she felt ashamed of herself and ashamed of her parents that they could have neglected their own kinsfolk; but the name must be spoken.

"Mildred Tingvold," she whispered, and burst into tears.

Aye, to be sure; none of the Tingvold family had he ever before of his own free will addressed. But what had now occurred was different from anything he had imagined; he fixed a pair of large eyes on her. There flitted through his memory the story about her mother's weeping like this in church on her wedding-day; perhaps it runs in the family, thought he, and felt a desire to get away from it.

"You must excuse me, if I have alarmed you," said he, and followed the dog; it was already bounding over the ridge.

When she ventured to raise her eyes, he had just neared the crest, and he turned and looked at her. It was but for a moment, for just then the dog barked on the other side; it startled him, he raised his gun and was off. Mildred remained motionless with her eyes fixed on the spot where he had stood, when a shot alarmed her. Could it be the bear? Could it have been so near her? And off she scrambled where *he* but now had climbed, and stood where he had stood, shading her eyes with her hand from the sun, and sure enough, half hidden by some brushwood, he was stooping over a large bear! Before she was aware of it she had sprung down to him; he beamed a smile on her, and he told her, speaking in a low, flexible voice, how it had all come to pass, that they had lost the scent, afterwards, though, found it here; he explained why the dog had been unable to scent the bear before he came close to his track; and amid this she had forgotten her tears and bashfulness, and he had drawn his knife. He wanted to skin the animal at once. The flesh was not worth anything at this time of year, he would bury it without delay; but the skin he wanted to take with him. And he requested her to help him, and before she knew what she was doing, she was holding while he was flaying; afterward she ran down to the sæter for an axe and a spade, and although she was afraid of the bear, and although it smelled vilely, she continued to help him until he was through. By this time it was past noon, and he invited himself to dine with her. He washed both himself and the hide, which was no easy task, and when he got through he sat down beside her in the sheeling; for *she*, to her shame, had not the dinner yet ready. He chatted away about one thing and another, easily and pleasantly, but in a very low tone, such as people are apt to use who have been much alone. Mildred gave the shortest answers she could; but when she sat right opposite him at the table, she could neither speak nor eat, so that they often sat in silence. When he had finished, he turned on his stool, and filled and lighted a short pipe. He, too, had become rather more taciturn than he had been, and presently he rose.

"I have a long walk home," said he, and as he gave her his hand, he added in still lower tones: "Do you sit every day where I found you to-day?"

He held her hand a moment as though awaiting an answer. She dared not look up, much less reply. Then she felt a hasty pressure of her hand. "Thank you for the day!" he said softly, and before she could gain command of herself, she saw him with the bear-skin over his shoulders, gun in hand, dog at his side, walking over the heather. She saw him outlined against the sky, as he reached the summit of the mountains; his light, brisk step bore him swiftly away; she stepped outside of the door and watched him until he had disappeared from view.

Now for the first time she perceived that her heart was throbbing so violently that she had to press her hands over it. A little while later she lay on the greensward with her face on her arm, and most accurately passed in review the occurrences of the day. She saw him emerge from among the young trees above where she sat; she saw him, with his broad shoulders and restless eyes, standing right in front of her; she felt the advantage he had over her, and her own alarm, and her disgraceful tears; she saw him on the crest of the ridge against the sun; she heard the shot, she was on her knees in front of him while he was skinning the bear; she heard over again every word he had uttered, and his low voice, which had so friendly a sound that it thrilled her through and through as she thought of it; she heard it again from the stool in front of the hearth, while she was cooking, and from the table while she was eating; she felt how she then no longer dared look him in the eyes, and she felt that she finally had embarrassed him too, for he had grown silent.

She heard him speak once again, as he took her hand, and she felt his grasp, — it thrilled her still from head to foot! She saw him crossing the heather, walking on and on! Would he ever come again? After the way she had conducted herself — impossible! Ah, how strong, beautiful, self-reliant was not all that she had seen of him, and how stupid and miserable was not all that he had seen of her! Yes, miserable, from her first scream at the dog to her blush of shame and her tears; from the clumsy assistance she gave him to the meal she was so long in getting ready for him! And to think she could not answer No, not even when he looked at her; and then, at last, when he asked if she sat every day at the foot of the ridge, that she did not say No, for she did not sit there every day! Did not her silence seem as if she were begging him, mutely imploring him to come and see? The whole of her pitiable helplessness — might it not be misconstrued in the same way? Ah, how mortified she was! There tingled a burning sense of shame through her whole body, especially in her face, as she buried it deeper and deeper; and then she conjured up the whole scene again, his magnificence and her wretchedness, whereupon her mortification increased.

When the bells announced the approach of the cattle she was still lying there, but now made haste to get ready for them. Beret, who came too, saw at once that there was something amiss; for Mildred addressed to her the most absurd questions and answers, and acted so stupidly that Beret several times stood still and stared at her! And when it was time for supper, and Mildred said that she could not eat, and instead of taking her seat at the table, sat down outside of the door, nothing was lacking to make Beret the exact picture of a hunting dog on the scent, but to have her ears point forward. Beret ate her supper and undressed — she and her sister slept in the same bed — and when Mildred did not join her she rose up softly many times and looked to see if her sister were still sitting at the door, and if she were alone. Yes, she sat there, and always alone. The clock struck eleven, then twelve, then one, and Mildred still sat outside, and Beret did not sleep. She pretended to be asleep, to be sure, when Mildred finally came, and Mildred moved very, very quietly; but after she got into bed Beret heard her sigh, she heard her say her customary evening prayer, so mournfully, heard her whisper: "Oh, help me in this, dear, dear God!"

"What does she want God to help her about?" thought Beret. She could not sleep; she heard her sister, too, vainly trying to arrange herself for sleep, now on one, now on the other side; she saw her at last give up entirely, push away the cover, and putting her hands under her head lie there staring before her, with wide open eyes. More she neither saw nor heard, for now she fell asleep. When she awoke the next morning, her sister was no longer in bed. Beret sprang up; the sun was already high in the heavens, the cattle had long been astir. She found her breakfast set aside, made haste to eat, then went out and found Mildred at work; but she was looking very haggard. Beret told her that she would at once find the cattle and go with them. The other made no reply, but she gave Beret a look that seemed to be intended to express her thanks. Beret pondered a few moments and then left.

Mildred looked around; yes, she was entirely alone. Then she made haste to get her milk vessels in order, the rest might be attended to as best it could. She washed herself, and brushed her hair, and then hastened into the sheeling to change her clothes, took her knitting and went toward the ridge.

She had none of the new strength of tne new day, for she had scarcely slept at all, and had eaten almost nothing for twenty-four hours. She walked as one in a dream, and it seemed as if she could not grasp a single clear idea until she reached the spot where she had been sitting on the previous day.

But she had no sooner taken her seat there than she thought: "If he should come and find me here, he must of course believe?" — Involuntarily she started up. Then she saw his dog on the ridge; it stood still a moment watching her, then came springing down toward her, wagging its tail. Every drop of blood in her body stood still. There! There he stood, with his gun, in the sun, just as the day before; he had come another way to-day! He smiled at her, hesitated a little, then climbed over the edge of the ridge and soon stood in front of her. She had given a little scream, and then had sunk into her seat. It was utterly impossible for her to rise again, her knitting fell from her hands, she turned her face away. He did not speak. But she heard him throw himself down on the grass just in front of her, with his eyes fixed on hers, and she saw the dog on the other side with its eyes resting on him. She felt that although she sat with her face averted, he could see it, could see her blushes. His hurried breathing quickened hers; she thought she felt his breath on her hand, but she dared not stir. She did not wish him to speak, and yet his silence was terrible. She could not help understanding why he sat there, and greater shame than that which overpowered her had never before been felt. But it was not right in him to come, and still worse was it for him to *be sitting here*. Then one of her hands was seized, and held tight, then the other; she *had* to turn a little at this, and with his kind, strong eyes and hand he drew her gently to him. She glided down on the grass at his side, so that her head fell on his shoulder. She felt him stroking her hair with one hand; but she dared not look up. Her whole conduct was supremely unbecoming, and so she burst into a violent fit of weeping.

"Aye, if you weep, I will laugh," said he; "for what has happened to us two is something both to laugh and cry over!"

But his voice quivered. And now he whispered into her ear that yesterday when he left her, he kept drawing continually nearer and nearer to her. This had increased to such a degree that when he reached his mountain hut he could do nothing but let the German, his associate, shift for himself, while he pushed on alone up the mountains. He had passed the night partly sitting, partly walking about on the heights; in the morning he had gone home to breakfast, but started off again forthwith. He was twenty-eight years old, and no small boy; but this he knew, that either the girl must be his or all would be lost. He wandered to the place where he had met her the day before, he did *not* expect to find her, he only thought he would sit down here by himself a while. When he saw her, he was at first startled, but then he thought that her feelings must be the same as his, and so he resolved at once to put her to the test, and when he saw that she really felt as he did, why then — yes, then — and he raised her head and she no longer wept, and his eyes glowed with such strange brilliancy that she was forced to gaze into them, and she blushed and bowed her head. But he went on talking, in his low, pleasant voice.

The sun shone on the tops of the trees that covered the slope, the birches quivered in a gentle breeze, the chattering of the birds blended with the babbling of a little brook that flowed over a stony bottom close by. Neither took note of the time that passed as they sat there together, it was the dog that first roused them. It had made several excursions around, stretching itself out in its place again after each one; but now it sprang barking down the hill. Both started up, stood a while and listened. But nothing could be seen. They looked again at each other, and then he took her up on his arm. She had never been carried since she was a child, and there was something in the act that made her utterly helpless. He was her defense, her future, her everlasting happiness, she must heed her instincts. Not a word was spoken. He held her, she clung to him. He bore her to the spot where she had first been sitting; there he seated himself and cautiously put her down at his side. She bowed her head lower than ever, that she might not be seen by him now that she had been thus dealt with. He was just about to turn to her when a voice right in front of them, called out, in tones of utter astonishment: "Mildred!"

It was Inga, who had followed in the track of the dog. Mildred sprang up; she gazed at her friend for an instant, then ran to her, put one arm about her neck and laid her head on her shoulder.

"Who is he?" whispered Inga, drawing her arm around her, and Mildred felt how she trembled.

But Mildred did not stir. Inga knew very well who he was, for she was acquainted with him; but she could not believe her own eyes! Then Hans drew nearer.

"I thought you knew me," said he calmly; "I am Hans Haugen."

At the sound of his voice, Mildred raised her head. He held out his hand; she walked up to him and took it, and looked at Inga with shame and joy blended in blushing confusion.

Hans took his gun and said farewell, whispering to Mildred as he did so, —

"You may be sure I will come soon again after this!"

Both girls accompanied him down to the dairy, and saw him walk away in the direction he had taken the day before. They watched him until he had disappeared from their sight. Mildred stood, leaning on Inga, and the latter felt that her friend could neither stir nor speak. But when Hans was quite out of sight, Mildred's head drooped on Inga's shoulder, and she said, —

"Ask me no questions, for I cannot tell you anything."

For a time she continued to nestle up against Inga, and then they went to the sheeling. There Mildred remembered that she had left everything in disorder behind her, and Inga now helped her. During their work they did not say much to each other; at all events, not about anything else than the work.

Mildred brought forward the noon-day repast, but could eat very little herself, although she felt the need of both food and sleep. Inga left her as soon as she could; she saw that Mildred preferred to be alone.

When Inga was gone, Mildred laid herself down on the bed and tried to sleep. Just once more, though, she wanted to single out from the day's occurrences something that he had said and that seemed to her the most delightful of all. In so doing she had occasion to ask herself what reply she had made to this. And then it became clear to her that she had not said one word — indeed, through their entire interview not a single word! She rose up in bed. He could not have gone many paces alone, before this must have occurred to him also; and what must he then have thought? That she was like one walking about in her sleep, or like a person utterly devoid of will. How could he long continue to be attracted to her. Indeed, it was not until he was away from her, in the first place, that he discovered his love for her; she trembled to think what discoveries he might make this day. Again, as on the preceding day, she sat down outside of the door. Through her whole life Mildred had been accustomed to take care of herself; she had led such a sheltered life. Therefore, in her entire behavior during the past twenty-four hours, she thought she had shown neither discretion nor consideration, scarcely even modesty. She knew nothing of such things, either from books or from real life; she saw with the vision of peasants, and no one has stricter rules of propriety. It is seemly, according to them, to suppress one's emotions; it is modest to be tardy in the expression of one's feelings. She, who beyond all others, had adhered to these rules throughout her whole life, and who, consequently, had enjoyed the esteem of all about her, had in one single day yielded herself entirely to a man she had never before seen! In the course of time he would be the very one who would most despise her! When it was a thing that could not be told, not even to Inga, what must it not be!

When Beret appeared at the first sound of the cattle bells in the distance, she found her sister lying outside of the sheeling, looking like one in whom there was no life. She stood by her until Mildred was compelled to raise her head and look at her. Mildred's eyes were red with weeping, her whole expression that of one who is suffering. But her countenance changed when she caught sight of Beret, for Beret's face showed traces of agitation

"What is the matter with you?" she exclaimed.

"Nothing!" replied Beret, and remained standing, with her eyes averted from Mildred, so that the latter had to drop hers, turn and rise to prepare for the evening meal.

They did not meet again until supper-time, when they sat facing each other. As Mildred was unable to eat more than a few spoonfuls herself, her eyes now and then wandered absently from one to the other at the table, but they rested chiefly on Beret, who seemed as if she would never get through. She was not eating, she was devouring her food like a hungry dog.

"Have you taken no food before, to-day?" asked Mildred.

"No," answered Beret, and continued eating.

Presently Mildred asked, —

"Have you not been with the herd-boys?"

"No," replied both she and the herd-boys.

In their presence Mildred would not ask any more questions, and later her own morbid mind made her quite unfit to take charge of her sister, and, as it seemed to her too, quite unworthy. This thought was but an addition to the growing reproaches, which were throbbing one by one through her soul, as she sat all the evening and into the night in her place outside of the sheeling door.

In the crimson flush of the evening, in the cold gray night, no peace, not the slightest inclination for sleep. The poor child had never before been in trouble. Ah, how she prayed! She would cease and begin again; she used prayers which she knew, and she poured out her soul in words of her own, and finally, totally exhausted, she sought her bed. There she again collected her thoughts; but her strength was all gone; she could only take up the burden of her prayer: "Help me! dear, dear God, oh, help me!" — and she kept repeating this, now in low tones, now aloud; for she was having a struggle within herself as to whether she should give him up or not. Suddenly she was so frightened that she gave a shriek; for quick as lightning Beret had darted up and was kneeling by her.

"Who is he?" she whispered, her large eyes flashing fire, and her heated face and short breath betokening great agitation of mind.

Mildred, overpowered by her self-torture, exhausted in soul and body, could make no reply; she had become so alarmed that she felt like sobbing aloud.

"Who is he?" repeated the other, in threatening tones, bringing her face nearer to Mildred's; "it is no use for you to hide it any longer; I was watching you two the whole time to-day!"

Mildred held up her arms, by way of defense, but Beret seized them and drew them down.

"Who is he, I say?" — this time she looked Mildred straight in the eyes.

"Beret, Beret!" wailed the other; "have I ever shown you anything but kindness since you were a little child? Why are you so unkind to me, now that I am in such distress?"

Beret let go of her arm, for Mildred was shedding tears. But Beret's breath was hot, and her heart throbbed as if it would burst.

"Is it Hans Haugen?" whispered she.

Breathless silence ensued.

"Yes," finally whispered Mildred, and burst into tears.

Then Beret drew down her sister's arm once more; — she wanted to look into her eyes.

"Why did you not tell me this, Mildred?" she asked, with the same burning zeal.

"Beret, indeed I did not know it myself,"

was the reply. "I never saw him in my life until yesterday. And no sooner had I seen him than I gave myself to him; that is just what torments me so that I feel as if I must die!"

"Did you never see him before yesterday?" screamed Beret, in the greatest astonishment.

"Never in my life," replied Mildred, vehemently. "Can you imagine so great a shame, Beret?"

But at this Beret flung herself over her, threw her arms about her neck, and kissed her over and over again.

"Dear, sweet Mildred, how delightful it is!" she whispered, all sparkling with delight. "Ah, how delightful it is!" she repeated, and kissed her. "And how I will keep the secret, Mildred!"—and she gave her sister a squeeze, then started up again. "And to think you believed I could not keep it to myself!" and she fell into sudden distress. "*I* not keep a secret when it concerned you, Mildred!" she began to cry. "Why have you forgotten me of late? Why have you put Inga in my place? Oh, what sorrow you have caused me! When you knew how fond I was of you, Mildred!" and she hid her face in her sister's bosom.

But Mildred now drew her arm round her and kissed her, and then assured her that she had not thought of this until now, and that she would never push her aside again, and that henceforth she would place implicit confidence in her, she was so good and true; — and she patted her, and Beret patted her in return. Beret rose up again on her knee; she wanted to see her sister's eyes in the glow of the summer night, which was already beginning to be tinged with the rosy flush of morning.

"Mildred, how handsome he is!" was Beret's first exultant shout. "How did he come? How did you first see him? What did he say? How did it happen?"

And what Mildred a few hours before believed she could never tell any one, she now found herself freely recounting to her sister; she was interrupted now and then by having Beret fling herself over her and give her a hug; but this only increased Mildred's delight in telling her story. They laughed and they wept; sleep had entirely escaped their minds. The sun found them thus: the one lying down, or resting on her elbow, transported by her own story; the other on her knees in front of her, with half parted lips, glittering eyes, and now and then flinging herself over her sister, in an exuberance of delight.

They rose together, and did their work together; and when they were through with it, and just for the sake of appearances had eaten their breakfast, they both dressed for the interview. He must surely come soon! The girls sat down in their holiday attire at the foot of the ridge, and Beret showed Mildred where *she* had been lying the day before; the dog had often come there to her. One sister's story followed swiftly upon that of the other; the weather too was fine to-day, only a few clouds were visible. They had soon chatted away the time beyond the hour when Hans was expected; but they continued to talk, and forgot it only to remember it again, and Beret sprang to her feet several times, and ran up to the crest to see if he were coming; but she neither saw nor heard anything of him. Both girls grew impatient, and Mildred suddenly became so to such a degree that Beret was alarmed. She represented to her sister that he was really not his own master; for two days the German had been left to fish and shoot and prepare his meals alone; that would scarcely answer three days in succession; and Mildred found that there was some justice in this.

"What do you think father and mother will say to this?" asked Beret, merely to divert her sister's thoughts.

But the moment she had uttered the words, she regretted having done so. Mildred grew pale and stared at Beret, who stared at her in return. Had Mildred never thought of this before? Yes, to be sure she had; but as one thinks of something far away. Fear at what Hans Haugen might think of her, shame at her own weakness and stupidity, had so completely absorbed her that she had thrust all else aside. Now the case was reversed; her parents suddenly and wholly occupied her thoughts!

Beret again strove to console her. When they saw him they would justify Mildred in what she had done; nor would they make *her* unhappy, who had been their joy; grandmother would help her too; no one could have any fault to find with Hans Haugen, and *he* would never give up!

All this rushed past Mildred, but she was thinking of something else, and in order to gain time to consider properly, she begged Beret to get the dinner ready. Beret walked slowly away, glancing over her shoulder several times.

Now what Mildred was pondering upon was: "Shall I tell father and mother about this at once?" Excited as she was from the tremendous strain of the day, the question grew to the size of a mountain. It seemed to her that she would be committing a sin if she received him now. She ought not to have engaged herself without her parents' consent; but she had been powerless to do otherwise. Now that it was done her only course was to seek her parents without delay! She rose to her feet, a light dawned in her soul. What was right must be done. When Hans appeared here again, she must have spoken to her parents. "Is not that so?" she queried, yet not exactly as a question; and "Yes!" she seemed to hear some one reply, although no one had spoken. She hastened to the dairy to tell Beret of this. But Beret was neither in the sheeling, nor in the dairy.

"Beret!" she called. "Beret! Beret!"

The echo repeated the name from every side; but it gave her no Beret. Round about she went searching for her sister without finding her. She had been agitated before, she was terrified now. Beret's wide-opened eyes, and the question: "What do you think father and mother will say to this?" kept growing larger and larger.

Could Beret have possibly gone to them herself? It would be just like her! Vehement as the child was, she would want to have the question decided, and Mildred consoled forthwith. Most assuredly she had gone!

But if Beret should be the first to carry this to her parents, they would misunderstand it; and Mildred struck briskly into the path leading to the parish! Once on the way she walked faster and faster, borne onward by ever-increasing excitement. She was not aware of this, only there was a buzzing in her head, a pressure about the heart, — she panted for breath. She was forced to sit down and rest awhile. But she could get no rest sitting, she must lie on the ground. She flung herself down on her arm, and thus she fell asleep.

For two days and nights she had scarcely slept or eaten, and what power this would naturally have over the soul and body of a child who had hitherto calmly and regularly taken her meals and slept in her father's house, she did not understand.

Now Beret had not gone to their parents but had started off after Hans Haugen! She had a long distance to go, and part of the way lay through an unknown region, along the edge of a wood, and later she had to go farther up the mountains, across plateaus that were not quite secure from wild beasts, which had been showing themselves about here of late. But she went bravely onward, for Hans must come, or it would be hard for Mildred: she scarcely knew her sister as she appeared now!

She was light-hearted and gay, her sister's adventure went tripping along with her. Hans Haugen was the most distinguished person she knew in this world, and Mildred deserved the most distinguished! It was no wonder that Mildred gave herself at once to him, no more than it was strange that he fell in love with Mildred at first sight. If their parents could not understand this they would have to do as they pleased, and these two must brave resistance as her great grandfather and her grandfather had done; — and she began to sing the bridal march of her family. It rang jubilantly out over the desert wastes and died away in the hazy atmosphere.

On the top of the mountain she paused and shouted hurrah! But a strip of the extreme and uppermost part of the parish was visible from where she stood; bordering on it she saw the last edge of the wood, beyond it the heath, and here where she was standing nothing but stones and rocky plains in rigid undulations. She sped swiftly onward in the buoyant air. She knew that the mountain hut must be situated in a direct line with yonder snow-capped mountain, whose peak towered above all the others, and pretty soon she was convinced that she had not very far to go. In order to make sure of her course she climbed upon a large loose stone, and then saw a mountain lake just below her. Whether it was a hut or a rock that she now saw beside the lake, she could not decide, for sometimes it seemed to resemble a hut, sometimes a rock. But close by a mountain lake his hut was said to stand. Yes, indeed, it was unquestionably by this very one, for there was a boat rounding yonder point! Two men sat in it; this must be he and the German. Down she sprang and started forward. But what she had thought so near, proved to be far away, and she ran and ran. The anticipation of meeting Hans Haugen excited her.

Hans Haugen sat secure in his boat with the German, unconscious of all the commotion he had caused. Hans had never been frightened himself. He was only happy, and he sat there making some verses for the bridal march.

He was no great poet; but he had put together something about their ride to church, and their meeting in the woods served for the refrain of each stanza. He was whistling and fishing and enjoying himself extremely; the Ger man was busy fishing and left him in peace.

They now heard shouting on the shore; both Hans and the bearded German raised their eyes and saw a young girl beckoning to them. They conferred together a moment, and then rowed to shore. Here Hans sprang out and moored the boat, and both men loaded themselves with the guns, coats, fish, and fishing tackle; but while the German went straight to the hut, Hans, with his burden, walked up to Beret, who was standing on a stone near by.

"Who are you?" asked he.

"Beret, Mildred's sister," said she.

He flushed crimson, and she did the same. But presently he grew pale.

"Is anything the matter?" cried he.

"No, nothing, except that you must come. She cannot bear to be alone now."

He stood still a moment gravely contemplating her. Then he turned and went toward the hut. The German had paused outside to hang up the fishing tackle; Hans now did the same, while the two exchanged some words. Inside of the hut, ever since Beret shouted, two dogs had been barking with all their might and main. The men went in together; but as they opened the door the dogs rushed out, Hans's and the German's, but were at once sternly recalled. All became still, and it was a long time before Hans came out again. But when he did appear, he wore other clothes than before, and he had his gun and his dog with him. The German accompanied him out. And they took each other by the hand, as though they were saying farewell for a long time. Hans at once approached Beret.

"Can you walk fast?" asked he.

"Yes, to be sure I can."

And he walked and she ran; the dog bounded along in front of them.

As it had not occurred to him that Mildred could feel less secure and happy over their betrothal than he himself had felt, this summons came to him as a message from a new world of thought. Of course, she was anxious about her parents! She was alarmed, too, at the haste in which everything had been brought to pass — to be sure she was! He understood this so well now that he was thoroughly astonished at himself for not having understood it before, — and he walked on! Why, even on him the meeting with Mildred had made an overwhelming impression; what must not she, a child, quiet and retired as the home of her parents, experience at being cast out in a storm? And he strode on!

During this rapid march Beret had skipped

along at his side, keeping her face, as far as possible, turned toward his. She had now and then caught a glimpse of his large eyes and flushed cheeks; but he was so completely encircled by his thoughts, that he had not seen her distinctly, and at last he lost sight of her altogether. He turned; she was a considerable distance behind him; but she was straining every nerve to keep up. She had been too proud to say that she could not endure such a march. But when he paused and waited until she came up, all out of breath, the tears started to her eyes.

"Ah! Am I walking too fast?" and he held out his hand as he spoke.

She was panting so that she could not answer.

"Let us sit down a little while," said he, and drew her toward him. "Come!" and he pulled her down into a seat at his side.

She grew rosier, if possible, than before; and she did not look at him. She was gasping as if she were losing her breath.

"I am so thirsty," was the first thing she could say.

They rose again, and he looked round; but there was no water near at hand.

"We must wait till we get on farther; then

we will find a brook," said he; "it would not be good for you to drink just now, either."

He sat down again and she took her seat on the stone in front of him.

"I *ran* all the way coming here," said she, by way of apology. "And I did not eat any dinner," she added presently; nor did I sleep any last night," she further volunteered.

Instead of expressing sympathy for her, he asked, hurriedly, —

"Then, I suppose, Mildred, too, ate no dinner, and, perhaps, did not sleep last night?"

"Why, Mildred did not sleep any the night before either, and she has not eaten, so far as I have noticed, no, not for" — she considered a while — "for ever so long."

He started up.

"Can you go on now?"

"Yes, I think I can."

And he took her by the hand, and the hurried tramp began anew. After a little while he saw that she could not continue at this rate, so he took off his jacket, gave it to her, and picking her up carried her. This she would not permit on any account. But he bore her lightly onward, and Beret held fast to his waistcoat-band; him she dared not touch. Presently she told him that now she was rested and could run very well. He put her down, took his jacket himself and hung it across his gun, and pushed on. When the brook was reached, they paused and rested a little before she drank. When she rose, he looked at her and smiled.

"You are a nice little girl," said he.

Evening was drawing near when they reached their journey's end. Mildred was sought in vain both in the dairy and on the ridge; their shouts died away in the distance and both were becoming alarmed, when Hans noticed that the dog was sniffing at something. They ran forward; it was Mildred's kerchief. Hans immediately gave a sign to the dog to seek the owner of the kerchief, and off the animal went! They followed over the mountain toward the other side, that is, in the direction toward the Tingvold region. Could she have gone home?

Beret told about her thoughtless question and its results, and Hans replied that he could well imagine that it would be so. Beret began to cry. Should they go after her or not? Beret chimed in: "Yes, yes!" she was quite distracted. Before starting they must go to the neighboring sæter to ask some one to look after the cattle. While they were still discussing this, all the time following the dog, they saw it pause and look back, wagging its tail. They ran forward and there they found Mildred!

She was lying on her arm, with her face half buried in the heather. They approached with soft steps, the dog licked her hand and cheek; she wiped the spots it had touched and changed her position, but slept on.

"Let her sleep!" whispered Hans; "and you go and meet the cattle; I hear the bells."

After Beret had started, he hastened after her.

"Bring some food with you when you come back," whispered he.

Now he seated himself at a short distance from Mildred, drew the dog to him, forced it to lie down, and sat there holding it, to prevent it from barking if a bird or some stray animal should stir near them.

The evening was cloudy; there was a gray light over the ridges and plateaus; all around was hushed; not so much as a little bird broke the stillness of the air. He sat or rather reclined with his hand on the dog. What should be agreed upon when Mildred awoke, he had quickly settled in his own mind. The future was without a cloud: he lay there gazing up at the sky, undisturbed by a shadow of anxiety.

He knew that their meeting was a miracle; God himself had told them they must walk through life together!

He busied himself once more with the bridal march; a suppressed joy reigned within his soul, he imprisoned his thoughts therein.

It must have been after eight o'clock when Beret came back, bringing food with her. Mildred was not yet awake. Beret put down her load, stood watching them a while, then seated herself, but at some distance from the others. They waited fully an hour more, during which Beret often jumped up to keep herself from falling asleep. Toward ten o'clock Mildred awoke. She turned several times, opened her eyes at last, saw where she was lying, sat up, looked at the others. She was half intoxicated with sleep, which kept her from clearly comprehending where she was and what she saw, till Hans rose, and smiling, approached her. Then she held out both hands towards him.

He sat down at her side.

"Now you have slept, Mildred."

"Yes, now I have slept."

"Now you are hungry."

"Yes, I am hungry." Here Beret drew near with the food.

Mildred looked at it and at them. "Have I slept long?" said she.

"Yes, you have. It must be nine o'clock. Look at the sun!"

Now for the first time she seemed to recall all that had occurred.

"Have you been here long?"

"Oh — no; but eat now!"

She began.

"You were on your way down to the valley?" inquired Hans, drawing his face nearer to hers.

She blushed.

"Yes," whispered she.

"To-morrow, when you have had your sleep *quite* out, we two will go down there together."

Her eyes were fastened on his; first wide-open and wondering, then smiling, filled with gratitude; but she said nothing. After this she seemed to revive. She asked Beret where *she* had been, and Beret told her she had gone in search of Hans, — and he told the rest. Mildred ate and listened, and it was evident that the old enchantment was gradually stealing over her again. She laughed merrily at hearing that the dog had found her and licked her face without waking her. The dog was sitting by, greedily watching every morsel she ate; now she began to share her meal with it.

As soon as she had finished, they went slowly

toward the sæter, and not long after Beret was in bed. The two others sat down outside of the door. There began to fall a drizzling rain, but as the roof projected they did not heed it. The fog closed about the dairy ; they sat as within a magic circle. The atmosphere was, consequently, more dark than light. Subdued words fell from their lips, each one bringing confidence. For the first time they could talk together. He tenderly begged her pardon for not having remembered that she might be differently constituted than he, and that she had parents to consult. She acknowledged her fright, and said that from the moment she had met him she had ceased to be herself ; indeed, she had even forgotten her parents. She no doubt had more to say, yet she would not continue. But in their trembling joy, everything spoke, even to the softest breath. The first delicate outpouring of soul to soul, which with others usually precedes and prepares the way for the first embrace, with these two followed it. The first true questions stole through the twilight, the first true answers floated back. Light as a breath, soft as down, the words fell on the air, and in the same way were wafted back. Thus it was that Mildred at last found the courage, softly, hesitatingly, to ask if he had not considered her conduct very strange. He assured her that it had not seemed so to him, no, not once. Had he not noticed that she had been silent throughout the entire interview yesterday? No, he had not observed it. Had he not thought — For a long time she failed to find words, but they came finally in a low whisper, and with averted face, — that she was very hasty in yielding to him? No, he had only thought how delightfully the whole thing had come to pass. But what did he think of her for crying, the first time he saw her? Well, he had not comprehended it then, but now he understood it very well, and he was glad that she was just as she was.

All these answers made her so happy that she longed to be alone. And as he had divined this too, he rose softly and bade her go to bed. She got up also. He nodded and went slowly to the stable, where he was to sleep; but she hastened into the sheeling, undressed herself, and not until she was in bed did she clasp her hands and thank God. Oh, how she thanked Him! She thanked Him for Hans, for his love, his forbearance, his charming nature; she could not find words for all she wanted to say; so she thanked God for all, all, everything, even for the pain of these two days; for how great had it not made her joy. She gave thanks for the solitude of the mountain, and prayed God to accompany her from these lofty heights down to her parents, then turned her thoughts again to Hans, and gave thanks for him, fervent thanks.

When she came out in the morning — Beret still slept — Hans was standing in the yard. The dog had had a whipping: it had disturbed a ptarmigan, and was now lying at its master's feet trying to curry favor with him. When Hans saw Mildred he released the dog; the delighted animal sprang up on him and on her, it barked a good-morning greeting, wagged its tail, and was the living expression of their bright, young happiness. Hans helped Mildred and the boys with the morning work, and when at last they sat down to breakfast, Beret too had risen. Every time Hans glanced at Beret she blushed, and when Mildred, after they had left the table, took hold of his watch-chain while she was talking with him, Beret hastened from the room. She was hard to find when they were ready to go.

"Listen, Mildred," said Hans, after they had gone a short distance, coming nearer to her and walking softly: "I have been thinking of something I did not find an opportunity to say to you yesterday."

His voice sounded so solemn that she raised her eyes to his face. He spoke slowly, and without looking at her.

"I wanted to ask you — if it is the will of God that we should be united — to come home to my house after the wedding."

She grew red, and after a while answered evasively, —

"What would father and mother say to that?"

He walked on for some time before he replied, —

"I did not suppose it would matter much to them if we two were agreed."

It was the first time his words had wounded her. She made no rejoinder. He seemed to be waiting for her to speak, and finally added more softly, —

"It is my wish that we two should be alone — that we might become used to each other."

Now she began to understand him better; but she could not yet find words. He walked on as before, slowly and without looking at her; he, too, was silent now. She felt oppressed and gave him a searching look. She saw that he was very pale.

"But, Hans!" she exclaimed, and paused, without being herself aware of it.

Hans also stood still, glanced hastily at her, and then at the gun he had rested on the ground and was now twirling round.

"Are not you willing to come home with me?"

His voice was smothered, but the gaze he fixed on her became suddenly full and steady.

"Yes, of course I am!" she hastened to reply.

Her eyes rested calmly in his, a flush mantled his cheeks, he shifted his gun to the left hand, extending the right to her.

"Thank you!" whispered he, and gave her hand a warm pressure.

They walked on.

The sole thought she gathered from this, she expatiated on in her own mind, and finally could no longer keep it to herself.

"You do not know my parents."

He walked on some moments before he replied, —

"No; but after you have come home with me, I will have time to become acquainted with them."

"They are so good," she added.

"So I have heard from every one."

He said this firmly but coldly.

Before she had time to think or speak again,

he began to tell her about *his* home, about his brothers and sisters, about the poverty they had all worked their way up from, about how capable, true, and cheerful his brothers and sisters were, about the summer visitors and the employment they furnished, about the buildings on the place, and especially the new house he would now erect, and which should be for themselves, and how she should have the supervision of everything, but also plenty of help; indeed, every one would be perfectly devoted to her, and he not least of all! While he was talking they quickened their pace; he spoke with warmth, came closer to her, and when he got through they were walking hand in hand.

Yes, truly; his love for his home and his people made an impression on her, and the unknown attracted, but there was something, nevertheless, something that seemed like a wrong to her own tender-hearted parents. She began therefore anew, —

"But, Hans! Mother is growing old and father is still older; they have suffered much — they need help; they have toiled hard, and" — She either would not or could not say more.

He slackened his speed and looked smiling at her.

"Mildred, you mean to say that the gard is intended for you?"

She flushed, but made no reply.

"Ah, well — sufficient unto the day is the evil thereof! But if they ever want to have us take their places, it is *they* who must request it of *us*."

He said this tenderly; but she knew very well all that it signified! Cautious as she was, and accustomed to consider the thoughts of others before her own, she submitted. But it was not long now before they got so far on their way that they could see Tingvold lying at their feet. And then her eyes wandered from the gard up to him, as though it should speak for itself! The broad, bright hill-slopes, encircled by the forest, the buildings, spread out so peacefully in the subdued sunshine, but so large and substantial, looked very beautiful. The valley lay below, the noisy stream meandered through it, gard after gard might be seen down on the plain, and on the opposite side of the valley, and gard after gard on *this* side; but none of them, not a single one, equal to Tingvold, none so fruitful, none so imposing to the eye, not one so sheltered in its own homelike comfort, and yet so sparkling on every side! When she saw that he was affected by the sight, she colored with pleasure.

"Yes," answered he, for she had actually asked a question! "Yes, it is true, Tingvold is a fine gard; it has scarcely its match." He smiled and bowed over her. "But I care more for you, Mildred, than for Tingvold; may I not hope that you, too, care more for me than for Tingvold?"

Since this was the way he took it, there was nothing left to her but silence. Moreover, he looked so happy, and he sat down, and she seated herself at his side.

"Now I will sing something for you," he whispered.

She felt happy.

"I have never heard you sing," said she.

"No, you have not; and although my singing is talked about a good deal, you must not expect anything remarkable, for all that there is about it is that I feel myself, *now*, I *must* sing."

And after sitting and meditating a while, he sang his bridal song to the tune of the family march. He sang very softly, but such an exultant tone she had never heard in any voice! The gard lay before her, the gard from which the procession would start; she followed the road with her eyes all the way to the bridge across the stream, then followed the road on the other side as far as the church, into the birch forest up on a hill, and the cluster of gards near at hand. The view was not a brilliant one, for the day was not clear; but thus it best suited the subdued vision of her dreams; for how many hundred times had she not taken this churchward journey in her thoughts, only she had not known with whom! The words and the tune enchanted her; the peculiar, warm, quiet voice stirred the depths of her nature; her eyes were full, but she did not weep, neither did she laugh; but with her hand in his she sat and looked, now at him, now at the landscape before her; and when while thus engaged the smoke curled up from the chimney at home at the first kindling of the fire that was to boil the noonday pot, she turned and pointed. Hans had just finished his song and now he also sat quietly gazing at the prospect.

A little while later, they were once more journeying onward through the birch forest, and Hans had some difficulty in keeping his dog still. Mildred's heart began to throb. Hans agreed with her that he would wait near by, and that she should go forward alone. He carried her over a few swampy places, and he felt that her hand was moist.

"Do not think about what you are going to say," he whispered; "just let the words come as they will of themselves."

She did not utter a word in reply, neither did she look at him. They emerged from the forest, which here consisted of tall, solemn firs, among which they had been slowly walking while he told her in a whisper about her great-grandfather's wooing of his father's sister Aslaug, marvelous stories which she only half heard, but which nevertheless gave her strength, —they emerged from the forest into the dawning light of the meadows and grain fields, and then even he became silent. Now she raised her eyes to his face, and her fear was so apparent and so great, that he became very anxious. He could find no words to bring to her aid, — the case was too fully his own. They walked side by side; some brushwood just opposite the house concealed them from the occupants. When they got so far that he thought she ought to go on alone, he whistled softly to his dog, and Mildred understood this to be a sign that they must part. She paused, looking so unhappy and desolate that he had to whisper, —

"I will pray for you here, Mildred; and then I will come when you need me."

Her eyes expressed her thanks, but not wholly, for she could neither think nor see clearly. And thus she went home. As soon as she had advanced beyond the bushes, she could see right into the large sitting-room in the main building, indeed, clean through it, for the room had windows on either side, overlooking both the forest above and the parish below. Hans, meanwhile, seated himself behind the nearest clump of bushes, with the dog at his side, and so he could see everything in the sitting-room as well as she; but the room was now unoccupied. She looked round once when she came to the barn; then he nodded to her. She turned the corner of the barn, and entered the farm-yard.

Here all was in the old accustomed order, and stillness reigned. Some hens were walking about on the barn-bridge. Up toward the store-house wall to the left the poles, used for drying hay and grain, had been brought forward since she went away; — she saw no other change. She longed to turn to the right to her grandmother's house; it was no doubt her fright that made her desire this respite before the interview with her parents; but there by the chopping-block between the two houses stood her father shafting an axe. He wore a knit jacket, with his suspenders outside. His head was bare; his long thin hair was blown over his face by the breeze that was just beginning to sweep up from the valley. He looked so well, almost cheerful over his work, that the sight of him inspired her with courage. He did not notice her, so quietly and cautiously had she come walking up over the chips.

"Good day!" she whispered.

He looked at her for a moment, in surprise.

"Dear me! Is that you? Is anything amiss?" he added hurriedly, and gazed searchingly into her face.

"No," said she, coloring slightly.

But his eyes remained fastened on hers, which she did not dare raise. He put aside his axe.

"Let us go in to mother," said he.

On the way to the house, he asked various questions in regard to the work at the sæter, and obtained satisfactory replies. "Now Hans sees us go in," thought Mildred, as they advanced through the opening between the barn and the store-house, on the other side. When they entered the house, her father went to the kitchen door and opened it.

"You will have to come in, mother," said he, through the door; "Mildred is here."

"Dear me! Is anything the matter?" was answered from the kitchen

"No," replied Mildred, from behind her father, coming forward to the door herself, and then going out to her mother, who sat in front of the hearth, peeling potatoes and putting them into the pot.

Mildred's mother now scrutinized her face as closely as her father had done, and with the same effect. Randi rose, and after setting aside the dish she held, she went to the opposide door, gave some orders outside, retraced her steps, took off her kitchen apron, washed her hands and came forward. They all repaired to the sitting-room.

Mildred knew her parents well, so she was sure that these preparations betokened that they themselves expected something more than common. Her courage had not been great before, and now it grew less. Her father sat down in the high seat, close by the farthest window, which faced the parish. Her mother had seated herself on the same bench, but nearer to the kitchen door. Mildred took her place on the first seat, that is to say, on the long bench in front of the table. Hans could see her there; he could also look right into her father's face, but he did not have so good a view of her mother.

Her mother asked, as the father had done before, about the sæter, obtained the same information and a little more, for she inquired more into particulars. Although it was evident that both parties were spinning out the conversation, the theme was soon exhausted. In the silence that ensued both parents looked at Mildred. She avoided their eyes, and inquired about the news of the parish. Although this theme was dragged out to the utmost, *it*, also, came to an end. Then the same silence, the same expectant look in the eyes of the parents. Mildred had no more questions to ask, but began stroking with the palm of her hand the bench on which she was sitting.

"Have you been to your grandmother's?" inquired the mother; she was beginning to be alarmed.

No, Mildred had not. This was an acknowledgment that she had come *here* on a definite errand, and she felt that it could be delayed no longer with propriety.

"There is something that it is my duty to tell you," the young girl faltered at last, her color coming and going and her eyes cast down. Her parents exchanged troubled glances. Mildred raised her head, and fixed on them a pair of wide-open, beseeching eyes.

"What is it, my child?" her mother anxiously asked, as she met her gaze.

"I am betrothed," said Mildred, bowing her head and bursting into tears.

A more stunning blow could not have fallen on the little circle! Pale, silent, the parents looked at each other. Their steady, gentle Mildred, for whose prudence and obedience they had so often thanked God, had, without their advice, without their knowledge, taken life's most important step, one which also determined the parents' past and future. Mildred, meanwhile, felt every thought that was working in their minds, and fear checked her tears. Gently, slowly, her father asked, —

"To whom, my child?"

After a pause the answer came in a whisper, —

"It is to Hans Haugen."

The name Haugen had not been mentioned in this house for more than twenty years, nor any circumstance connected therewith. From the stand-point the parents took, only harm had come from Haugen to this gard. Mildred again divined their thoughts; she sat motionless, awaiting her doom. But mildly and slowly once more the father said, —

"We do not know this man; neither your mother nor I. Nor were we aware that you knew him."

"No, neither did I know him," said Mildred.

The astonished parents looked at each other.

"How did this happen, then?"

It was the mother who spoke.

"Oh, I do not know myself," said Mildred.

"Why, dear child, we ought to be able to control our actions."

Mildred made no reply.

"We thought," added the father, meekly, "that we could trust *you*."

Mildred still made no reply.

"But how did it happen?" repeated the mother, more zealously. "You must surely know."

"No, I do not know. I only know that I could not help it; no, indeed, I could not. She sat clinging with both hands to the bench as she spoke.

"God have mercy on you, then! What can have come over you?"

Mildred made no reply. Once more the father had a subduing influence on the conversation. In a calm, friendly tone, he asked, —

"Why did you not speak to one of us, my child?"

The mother, too, fell into this vein, and said quietly, —

"You know how fond we are of our children, we, who have lived so lonely a life; and we may well say, of you, in especial, Mildred, for you have been dearer than all else to us."

Mildred scarcely knew where she was sitting.

"No, we did not think that you would forsake us thus."

It was the father who spoke. Hushed though his voice was, it pained none the less.

"I will not forsake you," she faltered.

"You must not say so," he answered, more gravely than he had yet spoken," for you have already left us."

Mildred felt that this was true, and yet it was *not* true; but she could not explain this. Her mother said, —

"Of what avail is it to us that we have led a loving, pious life with our children? At the first temptation" — For her daughter's sake she refrained from saying more.

But Mildred could not stand this any longer.

"I will not forsake you," she cried. "I do not want to grieve you. I only could not — no I could not!" and flinging herself down on the table with her face toward her father, and her head on her arm, she sobbed aloud.

Neither of her parents had the heart to increase with a single reproach the sorrow she evidently felt. Consequently a hush fell upon the room. It might have lasted a long time; but Hans Haugen noticed from his hiding-place that Mildred needed help. His huntsman's eye had seen her cast herself down on the table, and he sprang to his feet; soon his light step was heard in the passage. He knocked; every eye was fixed on the door; but no one said: "Come in!" Mildred half rose, her face red with weeping; the door opened, Hans, with his gun and dog, stood on the threshold, pale but calm, turned and closed the door, while the dog walked, wagging its tail, to Mildred. Hans' thoughts had been too much occupied to observe that the dog followed him.

"Good-day!" said he. Mildred sank back in her seat, drew a long breath, and looked at him, relieved; her fright, her bad conscience, was all gone, she *was right*, *yes*, *indeed*, *she was right*, — now God's will be done!

No one had responded to his greeting; nor had any one asked him to come forward.

"I am Hans Haugen," said he, calmly; and he rested his gun on the floor, and stood holding it. After the parents had exchanged glances a few times, he continued, but with an effort: "I came here with Mildred; for if she has done wrong, the fault is mine."

Something must be said; the mother looked at the father, and he said, finally, that this had come about without their knowledge, nor could Mildred give any explanation of how it had happened. But Hans replied that he could give none either.

"I am no boy," said he, "for I am twenty-eight years old, and yet this came about in such a way that I, who never thought of any one before, could not think of anything else in the world from the moment I saw her. Had she said no — ah, I do not know — but I certainly never would have amounted to very much afterward."

The calm, truthful way in which he said this, was good to hear; Mildred trembled in her seat, for she knew that his words presented a new view of the case. He had his cap on, for it was not customary in this valley for a stranger to take off his cap on entering a house; but now he involuntarily removed it, hung it on the barrel of his gun and held his hands over it. There was something in the young man's whole manner that demanded courtesy.

"Young as Mildred is," said the mother, "none of us thought that she would so soon begin to enter into anything of this sort."

"That may be true; but then you know I

am much older," replied he, "and the management of affairs at my house is not very extensive; it will not require great effort, and I have plenty of help."

The parents looked at each other, at Mildred, at him.

"Would she have to go home with you?" asked the father incredulously, almost scornfully.

"Yes," said Hans; "it is not the gard I am courting."

He flushed; Mildred did the same.

If the gard had sunk into the earth, it could not have astonished the parents more than to have it disdained, and Mildred's silence showed them that she agreed with Hans. At all events, this decision of the young people was something wholly beyond the calculations of the parents; they felt themselves humiliated.

"It was you who said you would not forsake us," remarked the mother in quiet reproach, and her words struck home.

But Hans came to Mildred's aid.

"Forsake you? Why, every child who marries must leave its parents." He smiled, and added, in a kindly tone, "The distance is not great; it is but little over five miles from here to Haugen."

Words, however, are of but little avail on sucn occasions; thoughts will take their course in spite of them. Mildred's parents felt forsaken, aye, betrayed, by the determination of the young people. That it was possible to live comfortably at Haugen they knew very well; travelers who visited the place had given it a name; there had even now and then been something about it in the papers; but still Haugen was Haugen, and that *Mildred*, their favorite child, should take the family's journey back to Haugen, it was too much! Under such circumstances others would perhaps have been angry, but these two preferred to avoid what they did not like. They exchanged significant looks, and the father said, mildly, —

"This is too much at once, we are unable to answer yet."

"No," joined in the mother; "we had not expected such important news; nor to receive it in this way."

Hans hesitated a little before he said, —

"It is true that Mildred should have asked her parents first. But how, if neither of us knew of it before it was too late? That is really the way it was. So we could not do anything else than come, both of us, as soon as we were engaged, and that we have done. You must not be too severe."

After this there was nothing to be said on the score of their conduct, and his calm way of speaking gave force to his words. On the whole, the father noticed that he was not an equal match to Hans, and so small was the confidence he had in himself he felt anxious to drop the question.

"We do not know you," said he, and looked at his wife; "we must have time to consider."

"Yes, that is certainly best," observed Randi, "for we ought to know the person to whom we give our daughter."

Mildred felt the indignity of this remark, but she looked imploringly at Hans.

"That is true," replied Hans, and began with one hand to twirl his gun, "although I do not think there are many in the parish who are very much better known than I. But perhaps some one has been speaking ill of me?"

He looked up at them. Mildred felt embarrassed for her parents, and they felt that they had possibly awakened suspicion, and this they did not wish.

"No, we have heard nothing against you," both exclaimed in a breath, and the mother hastened to add, that the fact was they did not know him because they had so seldom heard anything about the Haugen family.

She meant no harm in the least by this; but no sooner had the words crossed her lips than she realized that they were not happily expressed, and she noticed that both her husband and Mildred thought the same. There was some delay before the answer came.

"If the house of Tingvold has failed to inquire after the Haugen family, the fault is not ours; for we have been poor people until lately."

There was a reproach in these words that all three felt to be true, and that profoundly so. But never until now had it occurred to the husband and wife, reserved and absorbed in their sorrow as they had been, that they had neglected a duty; never until now had they considered that their poor relatives at Haugen should not have been made to suffer for misfortunes for which they were in nowise to blame. They stole shy glances at each other, and kept their seats, covered with shame. Hans had spoken cautiously, although the mother's answer could not but have annoyed him. Both parents felt then that they had a noble man before them, and that in a double sense they had something to make amends for. And so the father said, —

"Let us take a little more time. Cannot

you stay to dinner with us? Then we can have a chance to talk a little."

"You must come and sit down," added the mother.

Both rose.

Hans put aside his gun, with his cap on it, and crossed the floor to where Mildred sat; she at once rose, she knew not herself why. The mother said there was a good deal to be seen to in the kitchen, and left the room. The father acted as if he were about to follow her example; but Mildred, not wishing to be alone with Hans as long as her parents refused their consent, quickly moved to the other door. They saw her walking across the farm-yard toward her grandmother's dwelling. Then the father could not leave Hans alone, so he turned and sat down.

The two men talked together about indifferent matters; first of all about the hunting, and about their affairs on the mountain in the summer huts; about the income from such sources, and much more to like effect. Afterwards they came to Haugen and the tourists that found their way there, to the cultivation of the soil in these upland regions; and all that the father heard gave him the impression that everything was going on well and prosperously at Haugen. The mother, coming and going with her preparations for dinner, often had occasion to listen, and it was very evident that the shyness of the old people was gradually becoming transformed into confidence; for the questions began to grow more to the point.

They all noticed Hans's good manners at table. He sat at the wall, just opposite Mildred and her mother; while the father sat at the end of the table in the high seat. The farm people had had their dinner earlier, and in the kitchen where the family themselves usually ate with them. But the fact probably was that on this occasion they did not care to have Hans seen. At table Mildred felt that her mother looked at her whenever Hans smiled. He was one of those grave-looking people whose faces light up pleasantly when they smile. Several such things she put together to form the result her heart was set on having. But she felt so uncertain about matters that the atmosphere of suspense in the room was so oppresive to her, that she for her part longed to get away, and after dinner she went again to her grandmother's.

The men took a turn round the gard, but so directing their steps that they did not come either where the farm laborers were, or where the grandmother could see them. Later they sat down in the sitting-room again, and by this time the mother was through with her work and could join them. The conversation became by degrees more confidential, as might have been expected, and as time wore on (yet, to be sure, not before evening) the mother ventured to beg Hans to tell how it had all come about between him and Mildred, as Mildred had herself been unable to give any information. Perhaps it was chiefly feminine curiosity that led the mother to ask this, but to Hans the question was exceedingly welcome.

He gave no account of the first interview, for he could not do so; but in full details and with profound joy he narrated the events of the previous day, telling of Beret's stormy march in search of him, because Mildred was distracted with anguish of mind on her parents' account; and when he came to Mildred herself and depicted her flight toward home, and how, exhausted in soul and body, she had been compelled to rest, and had fallen asleep, desolate and unhappy, — then it seemed to the old people that they recognized their child once more. They could not avoid feeling, especially the mother, that they had been too severe.

But while the young man talked about Mildred, he was telling, without being aware of it, about himself; for his love for Mildred glowed from every word and made the parents glad. He grew conscious of this at last and became happy himself; and these two, who were unaccustomed to such unbroken heartiness and strength, felt genuine happiness. This kept continually increasing, until the mother involuntarily exclaimed, smiling, —

"Why, I really believe you got as far as the wedding, you two, before either of us were consulted."

The father chimed in with a laugh in order to help the question, and Hans replied, as seemed appropriate to the occasion, by softly humming a single line of the bridal march, —

"Speed us on, speed us on, we 're in haste, you and I," —

and laughed, but was discreet enough to turn the conversation at once to something else. By a mere chance he looked up at Randi and saw that she was very pale. In a moment he felt that he had done something wrong in reminding her of this tune, and that just now. Endrid looked anxiously at his wife, whose agitation kept increasing until it had risen to such a pitch that she could no longer remain in the room; she rose and went out.

"I am afraid I have done wrong," said Hans, in alarm.

Endrid made no reply. Thoroughly distressed, Hans rose to follow Mildred's mother and offer her an apology, but sat down again, protesting that he had not meant the least harm.

"Oh, you could not be expected to know," answered Endrid.

"Cannot you go after her and make all right again?"

He had acquired such confidence in this man that he felt at perfect liberty to ask this of him. But Endrid replied, —

"No; let her alone; I know her."

Hans, who had a little while before felt almost at the goal of his wishes, was now plunged in disappointment, and could not be coaxed into good spirits again, although the father exercised the utmost patience in trying to cheer him. The dog lent his aid, by coming forward and joining them, for Endrid had asked repeatedly about it and afterwards given a detailed account of a dog *he* had once owned, and whose ways he had closely observed, as solitary people are wont to do.

Now Randi had gone outside of the door, and seated herself on the flag-stone. Her daughter's betrothed had caused the bridal march to jar more than ever the memories she bore within her. *She* had not, like her daughter, given herself to a man whom she loved! The shame of her ride to church had been just, for she had not been sitting in perfect truth at her bridegroom's side. The mortification and grief, the loss of her children, the long years of suffering and conflict, all rushed over her. All she had read and prayed over this pain had then been of no avail, for the most violent agitation now overpowered her! That this could happen to her, cast her despairingly down into the depths of self-accusation; she felt the scorn of the people over her false churchward ride; she again scourged her own impotence, that she could not stop her tears that time, her memories now; that through her lack of self-control she had put her parents in a false light, destroyed her own health, and thereby murdered the children she bore,—all the time feigning a piety she did not feel, for she was sure of this now. Oh, to think she had progressed no farther than this! So wretched, so pitiably wretched she felt, that she did not dare look up to God; for how had she not disappointed herself and Him! But wherefore, she was forced to ask, wherefore call to light just now all the hatefulness that had coiled itself about her inner being? Was she envious of Mildred? Envious of her own daughter? No, she was not, she knew she was not, and she began to hold up her head once more! Now her sin should be atoned for by her daughter. What a glorious thought! Could our children atone for our sins? Yes, as truly as they are a work of our own, they could, for the truth that was in Mildred, the mother, frail as she was, had fostered. But in order to profit thereby she must enter into it herself in repentance, in gratitude! And before Randi knew how it was herself, she could pray again, could bend in profound humility and contrition before the Lord, who had once more revealed to her what she was without Him. She prayed for mercy, as those pray who are petitioning for their lives, for now she would have life again; this she felt! Now her debt was cancelled; this had been the final settlement, she was merely overwhelmed by it! And she rose and looked up, while the tears streamed down her cheeks: she felt at ease; there was One who had lifted her burden from her! But had she not often felt thus before? No, never as she did now; her first victory had just been won! And she advanced farther and she felt this: she belonged to herself! Something was rent asunder that until now had held her in bondage; through every motion she made she felt that now she was free, soul and body! If, next to God, she must thank her daughter for this, why, then, to Mildred must be granted the full enjoyment of her happiness! She came to the porch of grandmother's house; but none of those within recognized her step. She took hold of the latch and opened the door, as though she were another person.

"Mildred, come here!" said she, and Mildred and the grandmother looked at each other, for this surely was not Mildred's mother.

Mildred sprang forward. What could be the matter? Her mother drew her forward by the arm, closed the door behind her so that they were alone, and then flung herself on her daughter's neck and wept and wept, while she embraced her with vigor and an intensity of bliss, which Mildred, exalted by her love, could return with all her heart.

"God forever bless and reward you!" whispered her mother.

The two in the family sitting-room saw them coming walking across the yard, hand in hand, and they saw, moreover, that their coming was prophetic. The door was opened, they both entered and came forward. But instead of giving Mildred to Hans, or saying anything to the father or to him, Randi merely clasped her daughter in her arms again, and in a fresh burst of emotion, once more cried, —

"God forever bless and reward you!"

A little while later all four sat in the grandmother's room. The old lady was very happy; she had for a long time past been kept posted by the young people in regard to Hans Haugen, and she comprehended at once that this alliance would serve as an atonement in the lives of her son and daughter-in-law. Moreover, the light-hearted old lady thought Hans was extremely handsome! They all remained with her, and the day ended by the father, after singing a psalm, reading from a prayer-book a passage beginning: "The Lord has been in our house."

Of the remainder of their lives I shall only single out two days, and of these but a few moments in each.

The first is the wedding-day of the young people. Inga, Mildred's cousin, who was now herself a wife, had come to attend to the adornment of the bride. This was done in the storehouse; the old chest, in which the bridal silver was kept, — the crown, the belt, the buckle, the brooches, the rings, — was brought forward. Grandmother had the key to it, she was there herself to open it, and Beret was with her, as her assistant. Mildred had already decked herself in her bridal dress, and all the finery that belonged to her, when this splendor (which Beret and the grandmother had polished the week before) was brought to light, glittering and heavy. Article after article was tried on. Beret held the glass for the bride. The old lady told how so many of her family had worn this silver on their wedding-day, and how the happiest of all had been her own mother, Aslaug Haugen.

Just then the old family bridal march was heard outside: every one in the store-house paused, listened, then hastened to the door to see what was going on. The first person their eyes fell on was Endrid, the bride's father. He had seen Hans Haugen, and his brothers and sisters, come riding toward the gard; it was a rare thing for Endrid to have any unusual ideas; but this time it occurred to him that these guests should be received with the ancestral tune. He gave the fiddlers orders to go forward playing it; and there he now stood himself in their midst near the store-house, hold-

"Article after article was tried on" — Page 108.

ing in his hand a silver tankard filled with the wedding ale. Several others had joined him. Hans and his faithful brothers and sisters drove into the gard and it was very evident that this reception touched them.

An hour later, as a matter of course, the bridal march was struck up again; that was when the bride and bridegroom, and the bride's parents, and grandmother and Beret, and the bridegroom's brothers and sisters came out in couples, with the fiddlers at their head, to get into the carts. There are moments in our lives when all signs are favorable, and at such a moment the bridal party drove forth from Tingvold one bright spring day. At church there was assembled so great a multitude of people that no one remembered ever having seen anything to equal it. Every one in the crowd knew the family history, and how it was interwoven with this bridal march which now rang out jubilantly through the glad sunshine, its tones encircling the bride and bridegroom, and the happy bridal party.

And because all their thoughts centred in this one, the priest, too, chose a text for the wedding discourse that afforded him an opportunity of dwelling on the idea that children are the crowning glory of our lives when they are a reflection of *our* honor, our development, our labor.

On the way out of the church Hans paused in front of the church door; he said something; the bride, in her supreme happiness, did not hear what it was, but she divined its meaning. He wanted her to look at Ole Haugen's grave, which was richly decked with flowers. She did so, and they passed out of the churchyard in such a way that their garments touched the head-board of his grave. The parents followed.

The other moment of their lives which must here be unveiled, relates to the first visit of Endrid and Randi as grandparents. Hans had had his way, and the newly-married couple were established at Haugen, although he had been obliged to promise that he would take Tingvold when the old people either could not or did not wish to manage it longer, and when the ancient grandmother was dead. During this whole visit, however, there is but one occurrence that concerns the readers of this story; this is, that when Randi, after having been affectionately received and after partaking of the refreshments that were brought forward, sat with her daughter's little child in her lap, she began to rock it in her arms and hum something over it, and that was the bridal march. Her daughter clasped her hands in surprise, but controlled herself immediately, and said nothing. Hans invited Endrid to let him fill his glass again, which Endrid declined, but this was only an excuse on both sides to exchange glances.

THROND.

THERE was once a man named Alf, who had raised great expectations among his fellow-parishioners because he excelled most of them both in the work he accomplished and in the advice he gave. Now when this man was thirty years old, he went to live up the mountain and cleared a piece of land for farming, about fourteen miles from any settlement. Many people wondered how he could endure thus depending on himself for companionship, but they were still more astonished when, a few years later, a young girl from the valley, and one, too, who had been the gayest of the gay at all the social gatherings and dances of the parish, was willing to share his solitude.

This couple were called "the people in the wood," and the man was known by the name "Alf in the wood." People viewed him with inquisitive eyes when they met him at church or at work, because they did not understand him; but neither did he take the trouble to give them any explanation of his conduct. His wife was only seen in the parish twice, and on one of these occasions it was to present a child for baptism.

This child was a son, and he was called Thrond. When he grew larger his parents often talked about needing help, and as they could not afford to take a full-grown servant, they hired what they called "a half:" they brought into their house a girl of fourteen, who took care of the boy while the father and mother were busy in the field.

This girl was not the brightest person in the world, and the boy soon observed that his mother's words were easy to comprehend, but that it was hard to get at the meaning of what Ragnhild said. He never talked much with his father, and he was rather afraid of him, for the house had to be kept very quiet when he was at home.

One Christmas Eve — they were burning two candles on the table, and the father was drinking from a white flask — the father took the boy up in his arms and set him on his lap, looked him sternly in the eyes and exclaimed, —

"Ugh, boy!" Then he added more gently:

"Why, you are not so much afraid. Would you have the courage to listen to a story?"

The boy made no reply, but he looked full in his father's face. His father then told him about a man from Vaage, whose name was Blessom. This man was in Copenhagen for the purpose of getting the king's verdict in a law-suit he was engaged in, and he was detained so long that Christmas Eve overtook him there. Blessom was greatly annoyed at this, and as he was sauntering about the streets fancying himself at home, he saw a very large man, in a white, short coat, walking in front of him.

"How fast you are walking!" said Blessom.

"I have a long distance to go in order to get home this evening," replied the man.

"Where are you going?"

"To Vaage," answered the man, and walked on.

"Why, that is very nice," said Blessom, "for that is where I was going, too."

"Well, then, you may ride with me, if you will stand on the runners of my sledge," answered the man, and turned into a side street where his horse was standing.

He mounted his seat and looked over his shoulder at Blessom, who was just getting on the runners.

"You had better hold fast," said the stranger.

Blessom did as he was told, and it was well he did, for their journey was evidently not by land.

"It seems to me that you are driving on the water," cried Blessom.

"I am," said the man, and the spray whirled about them.

But after a while it seemed to Blessom their course no longer lay on the water.

"It seems to me we are moving through the air," said he.

"Yes, so we are," replied the stranger.

But when they had gone still farther, Blessom thought he recognized the parish they were driving through.

"Is not this Vaage?" cried he.

"Yes, now we are there," replied the stranger, and it seemed to Blessom that they had gone pretty fast.

"Thank you for the good ride," said he.

"Thanks to yourself," replied the man, and added, as he whipped up his horse, "Now you had better not look after me."

"No, indeed," thought Blessom, and started over the hills for home.

But just then so loud and terrible a crash

was heard behind him that it seemed as if the whole mountain must be tumbling down, and a bright light was shed over the surrounding landscape; he looked round and beheld the stranger in the white coat driving through the crackling flames into the open mountain, which was yawning wide to receive him, like some huge gate. Blessom felt somewhat strange in regard to his traveling companion; and thought he would look in another direction; but as he had turned his head so it remained, and never more could Blessom get it straight again.

The boy had never heard anything to equal this in all his life. He dared not ask his father for more, but early the next morning he asked his mother if she knew any stories. Yes, of course she did; but hers were chiefly about princesses who were in captivity for seven years, until the right prince came along. The boy believed that everything he heard or read about took place close around him.

He was about eight years old when the first stranger entered their door one winter evening. He had black hair, and this was something Thrond had never seen before. The stranger saluted them with a short "Good-evening!" and came forward. Thrond grew frightened and sat down on a cricket by the hearth. The mother asked the man to take a seat on the bench along the wall; he did so, and then the mother could examine his face more closely.

"Dear me! is not this Knud the fiddler?" cried she.

"Yes, to be sure it is. It has been a long time since I played at your wedding."

"Oh, yes; it is quite a while now. Have you been on a long journey?"

"I have been playing for Christmas, on the other side of the mountain. But half way down the slope I began to feel very badly, and I was obliged to come in here to rest."

The mother brought forward food for him; he sat down to the table, but did not say "in the name of Jesus," as the boy had been accustomed to hear. When he had finished eating, he got up from the table, and said, —

"Now I feel very comfortable; let me rest a little while."

And he was allowed to rest on Thrond's bed.

For Thrond a bed was made on the floor. As the boy lay there, he felt cold on the side that was turned away from the fire, and that was the left side. He discovered that it was because this side was exposed to the chill night air; for he was lying out in the wood. How came he in the wood? He got up and looked about him, and saw that there was fire burning a long distance off, and that he was actually alone in the wood. He longed to go home to the fire; but could not stir from the spot. Then a great fear overcame him; for wild beasts might be roaming about, trolls and ghosts might appear to him; he must get home to the fire; but he could not stir from the spot. Then his terror grew, he strove with all his might to gain self-control, and was at last able to cry, "Mother," and then he awoke.

"Dear child, you have had bad dreams," said she, and took him up.

A shudder ran through him, and he glanced round. The stranger was gone, and he dared not inquire after him.

His mother appeared in her black dress, and started for the parish. She came home with two new strangers, who also had black hair and who wore flat caps. They did not say "in the name of Jesus," when they ate, and they talked in low tones with the father. Afterward the latter and they went into the barn, and came out again with a large box, which the men carried between them. They placed it on a sled, and said farewell. Then the mother said: —

"Wait a little, and take with you the smaller box he brought here with him."

And she went in to get it. But one of the men said, —

"*He* can have that," and he pointed at Thrond.

"Use it as well as *he* who is now lying *here*," added the other stranger, pointing at the large box.

Then they both laughed and went on. Thrond looked at the little box which thus came into his possession.

"What is there in it?" asked he.

"Carry it in and find out," said the mother.

He did as he was told, but his mother helped him open it. Then a great joy lighted up his face; for he saw something very light and fine lying there.

"Take it up," said his mother.

He put just one finger down on it, but quickly drew it back again, in great alarm.

"It cries," said he.

"Have courage," said his mother, and he grasped it with his whole hand and drew it forth from the box.

He weighed it and turned it round, he laughed and felt of it.

"Dear me! what is it?" asked he, for it was as light as a toy.

"It is a fiddle."

This was the way that Thrond Alfson got his first violin.

The father could play a little, and he taught the boy how to handle the instrument; the mother could sing the tunes she remembered from her dancing days, and these the boy learned, but soon began to make new ones for himself. He played all the time he was not at his books; he played until his father once told him he was fading away before his eyes. All the boy had read and heard until that time was put into the fiddle. The tender, delicate string was his mother; the one that lay close beside it, and always accompanied his mother, was Ragnhild. The coarse string, which he seldom ventured to play on, was his father. But of the last solemn string he was half afraid, and he gave no name to it. When he played a wrong note on the E string, it was the cat; but when he took a wrong note on his father's string, it was the ox. The bow was Blessom, who drove from Copenhagen to Vaage in one night. And every tune he played represented something. The one containing the long solemn tones was his mother in her black dress. The one that jerked and skipped was like Moses, who stuttered and smote the rock with his staff. The one that had to be played quietly, with the bow moving lightly over the strings, was the hulder in yonder fog, calling together her cattle, where no one but herself could see.

But the music wafted him onward over the mountains, and a great yearning took possession of his soul. One day when his father told about a little boy who had been playing at the fair and who had earned a great deal of money, Throad waited for his mother in the kitchen and asked her softly if he could not go to the fair and play for people.

"Who ever heard of such a thing!" said his mother; but she immediately spoke to his father about it.

"He will get out into the world soon enough," answered the father; and he spoke in such a way that the mother did not ask again.

Shortly after this, the father and mother were talking at table about some new settlers who had recently moved up on the mountain and were about to be married. They had no fiddler for the wedding, the father said.

"Could not I be the fiddler?" whispered the boy, when he was alone in the kitchen once more with his mother.

"What, a little boy like you?" said she; but she went out to the barn where his father was and told him about it.

"He has never been in the parish," she added, "he has never seen a church."

"I should not think you would ask about such things," said Alf; but neither did he say anything more, and so the mother thought she had permission. Consequently she went over to the new settlers and offered the boy's services.

"The way he plays," said she, "no little boy has ever played before;" and the boy was to be allowed to come.

What joy there was at home! Thrond played from morning until evening and practiced new tunes; at night he dreamed about them: they bore him far over the hills, away to foreign lands, as though he were afloat on sailing clouds. His mother made a new suit of clothes for him; but his father would not take part in what was going on.

The last night he did not sleep, but thought out a new tune about the church which he had never seen. He was up early in the morning, and so was his mother, in order to get him his breakfast, but he could not eat. He put on his new clothes and took his fiddle in his hand, and it seemed to him as though a bright light were glowing before his eyes. His mother accompanied him out on the flag-stone, and stood watching him as he ascended the slopes; — it was the first time he had left home.

His father got quietly out of bed and walked to the window; he stood there following the boy with his eyes until he heard the mother out on the flag-stone, then he went back to bed and was lying down when she came in.

She kept stirring about him, as if she wanted to relieve her mind of something. And finally it came out: —

"I really think I must walk down to the church and see how things are going."

He made no reply, and therefore she considered the matter settled, dressed herself and started.

It was a glorious, sunny day, the boy walked rapidly onward; he listened to the song of the birds and saw the sun glittering among the foliage, while he proceeded on his way, with his fiddle under his arm. And when he reached the bride's house, he was still so occupied with his own thoughts, that he observed neither the bridal splendor nor the procession; he merely asked if they were about to start, and learned that they were. He walked on in advance with his fiddle, and he played the whole morning into it, and the tones he produced resounded through the trees.

"Will we soon see the church?" he asked over his shoulder.

For a long time he received only "No" for an answer, but at last some one said:

"As soon as you reach that crag yonder, you will see it."

He threw his newest tune into the fiddle, the bow danced on the strings, and he kept his eyes fixed intently before him. There lay the parish right in front of him!

The first thing he saw was a little light mist, curling like smoke on the opposite mountain side. His eyes wandered over the green meadow and the large houses, with windows which glistened beneath the scorching rays of the sun, like the glacier on a winter's day. The houses kept increasing in size, the windows in number, and here on one side of him lay the enormous red house, in front of which horses were tied; little children were playing on a hill, dogs were sitting watching them. But everywhere there penetrated a long, heavy tone, that shook him from head to foot, and everything he saw seemed to vibrate with that tone. Then suddenly he saw a large, straight house, with a tall, glittering staff reaching up to the skies. And below, a hundred windows blazed, so that the house seemed to be enveloped in flames.

This must be the church, the boy thought, and the music must come from it! Round about stood a vast multitude of people, and they all looked alike! He put them forthwith into relations with the church, and thus acquired a respect mingled with awe for the smallest child he saw.

"Now I must play," thought Thrond, and tried to do so.

But what was this? The fiddle had no longer any sound in it. There must be some defect in the strings; he examined, but could find none.

"Then it must be because I do not press on hard enough, and he drew his bow with a firmer hand; but the fiddle seemed as if it were cracked.

He changed the tune that was meant to represent the church into another, but with equally bad results; no music was produced, only squeaking and wailing. He felt the cold sweat start out over his face, he thought of all these wise people who were standing here and perhaps laughing him to scorn, this boy who at home could play so beautifully but who here failed to bring out a single tone!

"Thank God that mother is not here to see my shame!" said he softly to himself, as he played among the people; but lo! there she stood, in her black dress, and she shrank farther and farther away.

At that moment he beheld far up on the spire, the black-haired man who had given him the fiddle. "Give it back to me," he now shouted, laughing and stretching out his arms, and the spire went up and down with him, up and down. But the boy took the fiddle under one arm, screaming, "You shall not have it!" and turning, ran away from the people, beyond the houses, onward through meadow and field, until his strength forsook him, and then sank to the ground.

There he lay for a long time, with his face toward the earth, and when finally he looked round he saw and heard only God's infinite blue sky that floated above him, with its everlasting sough. This was so terrible to him that he had to turn his face to the ground again. When he raised his head once more his eyes fell on his fiddle, which lay at his side.

"This is all your fault!" shouted the boy, and seized the instrument with the intention of dashing it to pieces, but hesitated as he looked at it.

"We have had many a happy hour together," said he, then paused. Presently he said: "The strings must be severed, for they are worthless." And he took out a knife and cut. "Oh!" cried the E string, in a short, pained tone. The boy cut. "Oh!" wailed the next; but the boy cut. "Oh!" said the third, mournfully; and he paused at the fourth. A sharp pain seized him; that fourth string, to which he never dared give a name, he did not cut. Now a feeling came over him that it was not the fault of the strings that he was unable to play, and just then he saw his mother walking slowly up the slope toward where he was lying, that she might take him home with her. A greater fright than ever overcame him; he held the fiddle by the severed strings, sprang to his feet, and shouted down to her, —

"No, mother! I will not go home again until I can play what I have seen to-day."

A DANGEROUS WOOING.

WHEN Aslaug had become a grown-up girl, there was not much peace to be had at Huseby; for there the finest boys in the parish quarreled and fought night after night. It was worst of all on Saturday nights; but then old Knud Huseby never went to bed without keeping his leather breeches on, nor without having a birch stick by his bedside.

"If I have a daughter, I shall look after her, too," said old Huseby.

Thore Næset was only a houseman's son; nevertheless there were those who said that he was the one who came oftenest to see the gardman's daughter at Huseby. Old Knud did not like this, and declared also that it was not true, "for he had never seen him there." But people smiled slyly among themselves, and thought that had he searched in the corners of the room instead of fighting with all those who were making a noise and uproar in the middle of the floor, he would have found Thore.

Spring came and Aslaug went to the sæter with the cattle. Then, when the day was warm down in the valley, and the mountain rose cool above the haze, and when the bells tinkled, the shepherd dog barked, and Aslaug sang and blew the loor on the mountain side, then the hearts of the young fellows who were at work down on the meadow would ache, and the first Saturday night they all started up to the mountain sæter, one faster than the other. But still more rapidly did they come down again, for behind the door at the sæter there stood one who received each of them as he came, and gave him so sound a whipping that he forever afterward remembered the threat that followed it, —

"Come again another time and you shall have some more."

According to what these young fellows knew, there was only one in the parish who could use his fists in this way, and that was Thore Næset. And these rich gardmen's sons thought it was a shame that this houseman's son should cut them all out at the Huseby sæter.

So thought, also, old Knud, when the matter reached his ears, and said, moreover, that if there was nobody else who could tackle Thore, then he and his sons would try it. Knud, it is true, was growing old, but although he was nearly sixty, he would at times have a wrestle or two with his eldest son, when it was too dull for him at some party or other.

Up to the Huseby sæter there was but one road, and that led straight through the gard. The next Saturday evening, as Thore was going to the sæter, and was stealing on his tiptoes across the yard, a man rushed right at his breast as he came near the barn.

"What do you want of me?" said Thore, and knocked his assailant flat on the ground.

"That you shall soon find out," said another fellow from behind, giving Thore a blow on the back of the head. This was the brother of the former assailant.

"Here comes the third," said old Knud, rushing forward to join the fray.

The danger made Thore stronger. He was as limber as a willow and his blows left their marks. He dodged from one side to the other. Where the blows fell he was not, and where his opponents least expected blows from him, they got them. He was, however, at last completely beaten; but old Knud frequently said afterwards that a stouter fellow he had scarcely ever tackled. The fight was continued until blood flowed, but then Huseby cried, —

"Stop!" and added, "If you can manage to get by the Huseby wolf and his cubs next Saturday night, the girl shall be yours."

Thore dragged himself homeward as best he could; and as soon as he got home he went to bed.

At Huseby there was much talk about the fight; but everybody said, —

"What did he want there?"

There was one, however, who did not say so, and that was Aslaug. She had expected Thore that Saturday night, and when she heard what had taken place between him and her father, she sat down and had a good cry, saying to herself, —

"If I cannot have Thore, there will never be another happy day for me in this world."

Thore had to keep his bed all day Sunday; and Monday, too, he felt that he must do the same. Tuesday came, and it was such a beautiful day. It had rained during the night. The mountain was wet and green. The fragrance of the leaves was wafted in through the open window; down the mountain sides came the sound of the cow-bells, and some one was heard singing up in the glen. Had it not been for his mother, who was sitting in the room, Thore would have wept from impatient vexation.

Wednesday came and still Thore was in bed; but on Thursday he began to wonder whether he could not get well by Saturday; and on Friday he rose. He remembered well the words Aslaug's father had spoken: "If you can manage to get by the Huseby wolf and his cubs next Saturday, the girl shall be yours." He looked over toward the Huseby sæter again and again. "I cannot get more than another thrashing," thought Thore.

Up to the Huseby sæter there was but one road, as before stated; but a clever fellow might manage to get there, even if he did not take the beaten track. If he rowed out on the fjord below, and past the little tongue of land yonder, and thus reached the other side of the mountain, he might contrive to climb it, though it was so steep that a goat could scarcely venture there — and a goat is not very apt to be timid in climbing the mountains, you know.

Saturday came, and Thore stayed without doors all day long. The sunlight played upon the foliage, and every now and then an alluring song was heard from the mountains. As evening drew near, and the mist was stealing up the slope, he was still sitting outside of the door. He looked up the mountain, and all was still. He looked over toward the Huseby gard.

Then he pushed out his boat and rowed round the point of land.

Up at the sæter sat Aslaug, through with her day's work. She was thinking that Thore would not come this evening, but that there would come all the more in his stead. Presently she let loose the dog, but told no one whither she was going. She seated herself where she could look down into the valley; but a dense fog was rising, and, moreover, she felt little disposed to look down that way, for everything reminded her of what had occurred. So she moved, and without thinking what she was doing, she happened to go over to the other side of the mountain, and there she sat down and gazed out over the sea. There was so much peace in this far-reaching sea-view!

Then she felt like singing. She chose a song with long notes, and the music sounded far into the still night. She felt gladdened by it, and so she sang another verse. But then it seemed to her as if some one answered her from the glen far below. "Dear me, what can that be?" thought Aslaug. She went forward to the brink of the precipice, and threw her arms around a slender birch, which hung trembling over the steep. She looked down but saw nothing. The fjord lay silent and calm. Not even a bird ruffled its smooth surface. Aslaug sat down and began singing again. Then she was sure that some one responded with the same tune and nearer than the first time. "It must be somebody, after all." Aslaug sprang up and bent out over the brink of the steep; and there, down at the foot of a rocky wall, she saw a boat moored, and it was so far down that it appeared like a tiny shell. She looked a little farther up, and her eyes fell on a red cap, and under the cap she saw a young man, who was working his way up the almost perpendicular side of the mountain. "Dear me, who can that be?" asked Aslaug, as she let go of the birch and sprang far back.

She dared not answer her own question, for she knew very well who it was. She threw herself down on the greensward and took hold of the grass with both hands, as though it were *she* who must not let go her hold. But the grass came up by the roots.

She cried aloud and prayed God to help Thore. But then it struck her that this conduct of Thore's was really tempting God, and therefore no help could be expected.

"Just this once!" she implored.

And she threw her arms around the dog, as if it were Thore she were keeping from loosing his hold. She rolled over the grass with him, and the moments seemed years. But then the dog tore himself away. "Bow-bow," he barked over the brink of the steep and wagged his tail. "Bow-wow," he barked at Aslaug, and threw his forepaws up on her. "Bow-wow," over the precipice again; and a red cap appeared over the brow of the mountain and Thore lay in her arms.

Now when old Knud Huseby heard of this, he made a very sensible remark, for he said, —

"That boy is worth having; the girl shall be his."

THE BEAR HUNTER.

A worse boy to tell lies than the priest's oldest son could scarcely be found in the whole parish; he was also a very good reader; there was no lack on that score, and what he read the peasants were glad to hear, but when it was something they were well pleased with, he would make up more of the same kind, as much as he thought they wanted. His own stories were mostly about strong men and about love.

Soon the priest noticed that the threshing up in the barn was being done in a more and more lazy manner; he went to see what the matter was, and behold it was Thorvald, who stood there telling stories. Soon the quantity of wood brought home from the forest became wonderfully small; he went to see what the trouble was, and there stood Thorvald again, telling stories. There must be an end to this, thought the priest; and he sent the boy to the nearest school.

Only peasant children attended this school, but the priest thought it would be too expensive to keep a private tutor for this one boy. But Thorvald had not been a week among the scholars, before one of his schoolmates came in pale as a corpse, and said he had met some of the underground folk coming along the road. Another boy, still paler, followed, and said that he had actually seen a man without a head walking about and moving the boats down by the landing-place. And what was worst of all, little Knud Pladsen and his young sister, one evening, as they were returning home from school, came running back, almost out of their senses, crying, and declaring that they had heard the bear up near the parsonage; nay, little Marit had even seen his gray eyes sparkle. But now the school-master got terribly angry, struck the table with his ferule, and asked what the deuce — God pardon me my wicked sin — had gotten into the school-children.

"One is growing more crazy than the other," said he. "There lurks a hulder in every bush; there sits a merman under every boat; the bear is out in midwinter! Have you no more faith in your God or in your catechism," quoth he, "or do you believe in all kinds of deviltry, and in all the terrible powers of darkness, and in bears roaming about in the middle of winter?"

But then he calmed down somewhat after a while, and asked little Marit whether she really did not dare to go home. The child sobbed and cried, and declared that it was utterly impossible. The school-master then said that Thorvald, who was the eldest of those remaining, should go with her through the wood.

"No, he has seen the bear himself," cried Marit; " it was he who told us about it."

Thorvald shrank within himself, where he was sitting, especially when the school-master looked at him and drew the ferule affectionately through his left hand.

"Have you seen the bear?" he asked, quietly.

"Well, at any rate, I know," said Thorvald, "that our overseer found a bear's den up in the priest's wood, the day he was out ptarmigan shooting."

"But have you seen the bear yourself?"

"It was not one, it was two large ones, and perhaps there were two smaller ones besides, as the old ones generally have their last year's cubs and this year's, too, with them."

"But have *you* seen them?" reiterated the school-master, still more mildly, as he kept drawing the ferule between his fingers.

Thorvald was silent for a moment.

"I saw the bear that Lars, the hunter, felled last year, at any rate."

Then the school-master came a step nearer, and asked, so pleasantly that the boy became frightened, —

"Have you seen the bears up in the parsonage wood, I ask?"

Thorvald did not say another word.

"Perhaps your memory did not serve you quite right this time?" said the school-master, taking the boy by the jacket collar and striking his own side with the ferule.

Thorvald did not say a word; the other children dared not look that way. Then the school-master said earnestly, —

"It is wicked for a priest's son to tell lies, and still more wicked to teach the poor peasant children to do such things."

And so the boy escaped for that time

But the next day at school (the teacher had been called up to the priest's and the children were left to themselves) Marit was the first one to ask Thorvald to tell her something about the bear again.

"But you get so frightened," said he.

"Oh, I think I will have to stand it," said she, and moved closer to her brother.

"Ah, now you had better believe it will be shot!" said Thorvald, and nodded his head. "There has come a fellow to the parish who is able to shoot it. No sooner had Lars, the hunter, heard about the bear's den up in the parsonage wood, than he came running through seven whole parishes with a rifle as heavy as the upper mill-stone, and as long as from here to Hans Volden, who sits yonder."

"Mercy!" cried all the children.

"As long?" repeated Thorvald; "yes, it is certainly as long as from here to yonder bench."

"Have you seen it?" asked Ole Böen.

"Have I seen it, do you say? Why, I have been helping to clean it, and that is what Lars will not allow everybody to do, let me tell you. Of course *I* could not lift it, but that made no difference; I only cleaned the lock, and that is not the easiest work, I can tell you."

"People say that gun of Lars's has taken to missing its mark of late," said Hans Volden, leaning back, with both his feet on the desk. "Ever since that time when Lars shot, up at Osmark, at a bear that was asleep, it misses fire twice and misses the mark the third time."

"Yes, ever since he shot at a bear that was asleep," chimed in the girls.

"The fool!" added the boys.

"There is only one way in which this difficulty with the rifle can be remedied," said Ole Böen, "and that is to thrust a living snake down its barrel."

"Yes, we all know that," said the girls. They wanted to hear something new.

"It is now winter, and snakes are not to be found, and so Lars cannot depend very much upon his rifle," said Hans Volden, thoughtfully.

"He wants Niels Böen along with him, does he not?" asked Thorvald.

"Yes," said the boy from Böen's, who was, of course, best posted in regard to this; "but Niels will get permission neither from his mother nor from his sister. His father certainly died from the wrestle he had with the bear up at the sæter last year, and now they have no one but Niels."

"Is it so dangerous, then?" asked a little boy.

"Dangerous?" cried Thorvald. "The bear has as much sense as ten men, and as much strength as twelve."

"Yes, we know that," said the girls once more. They were bent on hearing something new.

"But Niels is like his father; I dare say he will go along," continued Thorvald.

"Of course he will go along," said Ole Böen; "this morning early, before any one was stirring over yonder at our gard, I saw Niels Böen, Lars the hunter, and one man more, going up the mountain with their rifles. I should not be surprised if they were going to the parsonage wood."

"Was it early?" asked the children, in concert.

"Very early! I was up before mother, and started the fire."

"Did Lars have the long rifle?" asked Hans.

"That I do not know, but the one he had was as long as from here to the chair."

"Oh, what a story!" said Thorvald.

"Why, you said so yourself," answered Ole.

"No, the long rifle which I saw, he will scarcely use any more."

"Well, this one was, at all events, as long — as long — as from here, nearly over to the chair."

"Ah! perhaps he had it with him then, after all."

"Just think," said Marit, "now they are up among the bears."

"And at this very moment they may be in a fight," said Thorvald.

Then followed a deep, nay, almost solemn silence.

"I think I will go," said Thorvald, taking his cap.

"Yes! yes! then you will find out something," shouted all the rest, and they became full of life again.

"But the school-master?" said he, and stopped.

"Nonsense! you are the priest's son," said Ole Böen.

"Yes, if the school-master touches me with a finger!" said Thorvald, with a significant nod, in the midst of the deep silence of the rest.

"Will you hit him back?" asked they, eagerly.

"Who knows?" said Thorvald, nodding, and went away.

They thought it best to study while he was gone, but none of them were able to do so,— they had to keep talking about the bear. They began guessing how the affair would turn out. Hans bet with Ole that Lars's rifle had missed fire, and that the bear had sprung at him. Little Knud Pladsen thought they had all fared badly, and the girls took his side. But there came Thorvald.

"Let us go," said he, as he pulled open the door, so excited that he could scarcely speak.

"But the school-master?" asked some of the children.

"The deuce take the school-master! The bear! The bear!" cried Thorvald, and could say no more.

"Is it shot?" asked one, very softly, and the others dared not draw their breath.

Thorvald sat panting for a while, finally he got up, mounted one of the benches, swung his cap, and shouted, —

"Let us go, I say. I will take all the responsibility."

"But where shall we go?" asked Hans.

"The largest bear has been borne down, the others still remain. Niels Böen has been badly hurt, because Lars's rifle missed its mark, and the bears rushed straight at them. The boy who went with them saved himself only by throwing himself flat on the ground, and pretending to be dead, and the bear did not touch him. As soon as Lars and Niels had killed their bear, they shot his also. Hurrah!"

"Hurrah!" shouted all, both girls and boys, and up from their seats, and out through the door, they sprang, and off they ran over field and wood to Böen, as though there was no such thing as a school-master in the whole world.

The girls soon complained that they were not able to keep up, but the boys took them by the hand and away they all rushed.

"Take care not to touch it!" said Thorvald; "it sometimes happens that the bears become alive again."

"Is that so?" asked Marit.

"Yes, and they appear in a new form, so have a care!"

And they kept running.

"Lars shot the largest one ten times before it fell," he began again.

"Just think! ten times!"

And they kept running.

"And Niels stabbed it eighteen times with his knife before it fell!"

"Mercy! what a bear!"

And the children ran so that the sweat poured down from their faces.

Finally they reached the place. Ole Böen pushed the door open and got in first.

"Have a care!" cried Hans after him.

Marit and a little girl that Thorvald and Hans had led between them, were the next ones, and then came Thorvald, who did not go far forward, but remained standing where he could observe the whole scene.

"See the blood!" said he to Hans.

The others hardly knew whether they should venture in just yet.

"Do you see it?" asked a girl of a boy, who stood by her side in the door.

Yes, it is as large as the captain's large horse," answered he, and went on talking to her. It was bound with iron chains, he said, and had even broken the one that had been put about its fore-legs. He could see distinctly that it was alive, and the blood was flowing from it like a waterfall.

Of course, this was not true; but they forgot that when they caught sight of the bear, the rifle, and Niels, who sat there with bandaged wounds after the fight with the bear, and when they heard old Lars the hunter tell how all had happened. So eagerly, and with so much interest did they look and listen, that they did not observe that some one came behind them who also began to tell his story, and that in the following manner: —

"I will teach you to leave the school without my permission, that I will!"

A cry of fright arose from the whole crowd, and out through the door, through the veranda, and out into the yard they ran. Soon they appeared like a lot of black balls, rolling one by one, over the snow-white field, and when the school-master on his old legs followed them to the school-house, he could hear the children reading from afar off; they read until the walls fairly rattled.

Aye, that was a glorious day, the day when the bear-hunter came home! It began in sunshine and ended in rain, but such days are usuallv the best growing days.

THE FATHER.

THE man whose story is here to be told was the wealthiest and most influential person in his parish; his name was Thord Överaas. He appeared in the priest's study one day, tall and earnest.

"I have gotten a son," said he, "and I wish to present him for baptism."

"What shall his name be?"

"Finn, — after my father."

"And the sponsors?"

They were mentioned, and proved to be the best men and women of Thord's relations in the parish.

"Is there anything else?" inquired the priest, and looked up.

The peasant hesitated a little.

"I should like very much to have him baptized by himself," said he, finally.

"That is to say on a week-day?"

"Next Saturday, at twelve o'clock noon."

"Is there anything else?" inquired the priest.

"There is nothing else;" and the peasant twirled his cap, as though he were about to go.

Then the priest rose. "There is yet this, however," said he, and walking toward Thord, he took him by the hand and looked gravely into his eyes: "God grant that the child may become a blessing to you!"

One day sixteen years later, Thord stood once more in the priest's study.

"Really, you carry your age astonishingly well, Thord," said the priest; for he saw no change whatever in the man.

"That is because I have no troubles," replied Thord.

To this the priest said nothing, but after a while he asked: "What is your pleasure this evening?"

"I have come this evening about that son of mine who is to be confirmed to-morrow."

"He is a bright boy."

"I did not wish to pay the priest until I heard what number the boy would have when he takes his place in church to-morrow."

"He will stand number one."

"So I have heard; and here are ten dollars for the priest."

"Is there anything else I can do for you?" inquired the priest, fixing his eyes on Thord.

"There is nothing else."

Thord went out.

Eight years more rolled by, and then one day a noise was heard outside of the priest's study, for many men were approaching, and at their head was Thord, who entered first.

The priest looked up and recognized him.

"You come well attended this evening, Thord," said he.

"I am here to request that the bans may be published for my son: he is about to marry Karen Storliden, daughter of Gudmund, who stands here beside me."

"Why, that is the richest girl in the parish."

"So they say," replied the peasant, stroking back his hair with one hand.

The priest sat a while as if in deep thought, then entered the names in his book, without making any comments, and the men wrote their signatures underneath. Thord laid three dollars on the table.

"One is all I am to have," said the priest.

"I know that very well; but he is my only child; I want to do it handsomely."

The priest took the money

"This is now the third time, Thord, that you have come here on your son's account."

"But now I am through with him," said Thord, and folding up his pocket-book he said farewell and walked away.

The men slowly followed him.

A fortnight later, the father and son were rowing across the lake, one calm, still day, to Storliden to make arrangements for the wedding.

"This thwart is not secure," said the son, and stood up to straighten the seat on which he was sitting.

At the same moment the board he was standing on slipped from under him; he threw out his arms, uttered a shriek, and fell overboard.

"Take hold of the oar!" shouted the father, springing to his feet and holding out the oar.

But when the son had made a couple of efforts he grew stiff.

"Wait a moment!" cried the father, and began to row toward his son.

Then the son rolled over on his back, gave his father one long look, and sank.

Thord could scarcely believe it; he held the boat still, and stared at the spot where his son had gone down, as though he must surely come to the surface again. There rose some bubbles, then some more, and finally one large one that burst; and the lake lay there as smooth and bright as a mirror again.

For three days and three nights people saw the father rowing round and round the spot, without taking either food or sleep; he was dragging the lake for the body of his son. And toward morning of the third day he found it, and carried it in his arms up over the hills to his gard.

It might have been about a year from that day, when the priest, late one autumn evening, heard some one in the passage outside of the door, carefully trying to find the latch. The priest opened the door, and in walked a tall, thin man, with bowed form and white hair. The priest looked long at him before he recognized him. It was Thord.

"Are you out walking so late?" said the priest, and stood still in front of him.

"Ah, yes! it is late." said Thord, and took a seat.

The priest sat down also, as though waiting. A long, long silence followed. At last Thord said, —

"I have something with me that I should like to give to the poor; I want it to be invested as a legacy in my son's name."

He rose, laid some money on the table, and sat down again. The priest counted it.

"It is a great deal of money," said he.

"It is half the price of my gard. I sold it to-day."

The priest sat long in silence. At last he asked, but gently, —

"What do you propose to do now, Thord?"

"Something better."

They sat there for a while, Thord with downcast eyes, the priest with his eyes fixed on Thord. Presently the priest said, slowly and softly, —

"I think your son has at last brought you a true blessing."

"Yes, I think so myself," said Thord, looking up, while two big tears coursed slowly down his cheeks.

THE EAGLE'S NEST.

THE Endregards was the name of a small solitary parish, surrounded by lofty mountains. It lay in a flat and fertile valley, and was intersected by a broad river that flowed down from the mountains. This river emptied into a lake, which was situated close by the parish, and presented a fine view of the surrounding country.

Up the Endre-Lake the man had come rowing, who had first cleared this valley ; his name was Endre, and it was his descendants who dwelt here. Some said he had fled hither on account of a murder he had committed, and that was why his family were so dark ; others said this was on account of the mountains, which shut out the sun at five o'clock of a midsummer afternoon.

Over this parish there hung an eagle's nest. It was built on a cliff far up the mountains ; all could see the mother eagle alight in her nest, but no one could reach it. The male eagle went sailing over the parish, now swooping down after a lamb, now after a kid; once he had also taken a little child and borne it away; therefore there was no safety in the parish as long as the eagle had a nest in this mountain. There was a tradition among the people, that in old times there were two brothers who had climbed up to the nest and torn it down; but nowadays there was no one who was able to reach it.

Whenever two met at the Endregards, they talked about the eagle's nest, and looked up. Every one knew, when the eagles reappeared in the new year, where they had swooped down and done mischief, and who had last endeavored to reach the nest. The youth of the place, from early boyhood, practiced climbing mountains and trees, wrestling and scuffling, in order that one day they might reach the cliff and demolish the nest, as those two brothers had done.

At the time of which this story tells, the best boy at the Endregards was named Leif, and he was not of the Endre family. He had curly hair and small eyes, was clever in all play, and was fond of the fair sex. He early said of himself, that one day he would reach the eagle's nest; but old people remarked that he should not have said so aloud.

This annoyed him, and even before he had reached his prime he made the ascent. It was one bright Sunday forenoon, early in the summer; the young eagles must be just about hatched. A vast multitude of people had gathered together at the foot of the mountain to behold the feat; the old people advising him against attempting it, the young ones urging him on.

But he hearkened only to his own desires, and waiting until the mother eagle left her nest, he gave one spring into the air, and hung in a tree several yards from the ground. The tree grew in a cleft in the rock, and from this cleft he began to climb upward. Small stones loosened under his feet, earth and gravel came rolling down, otherwise all was still, save for the stream flowing behind, with its suppressed, ceaseless murmur. Soon he had reached a point where the mountain began to project; here he hung long by one hand, while his foot groped for a sure resting-place, for he could not see. Many, especially women, turned away, saying he would never have done this had he had parents living. He found footing at last, however, sought again, now with the hand, now with the foot, failed, slipped, then hung fast again. They who stood below could hear one another breathing.

Suddenly there rose to her feet, a tall, young girl, who had been sitting on a stone apart from the rest; it was said that she had been betrothed to Leif from early childhood, although he was not of her kindred. Stretching out her arms she called aloud: "Leif, Leif, why do you do this?" Every eye was turned on her. Her father, who was standing close by, gave her a stern look, but she heeded him not. "Come down again, Leif," she cried; "I love you, and there is nothing to be gained up there!"

They could see that he was considering; he hesitated a moment or two, and then started onward. For a long time all went well, for he was sure-footed and had a strong grip; but after a while it seemed as if he were growing weary, for he often paused. Presently a little stone came rolling down as a harbinger, and every one who stood there had to watch its course to the bottom. Some could endure it no longer, and went away. The girl alone still stood on the stone, and wringing her hands continued to gaze upward.

Once more Leif took hold with one hand;

but it slipped; she saw this distinctly; then he tried the other; it slipped also. "Leif!" she shouted, so loud that her voice rang through the mountains, and all the others chimed in with her. "He is slipping!" they cried, and stretched up their hands to him, both men and women. He was indeed slipping, carrying with him sand, stones, and earth; slipping, continually slipping, ever faster and faster. The people turned away, and then they heard a rustling and scraping in the mountain behind them, after which, something fell with a heavy thud, like a great piece of wet earth.

When they could look round again, he was lying there crushed and mutilated beyond recognition. The girl had fallen down on the stone, and her father took her up in his arms and bore her away.

The youths who had taken the most pains to incite Leif to the perilous ascent now dared not lend a hand to pick him up; some were even unable to look at him. So the old people had to go forward. The eldest of them, as he took hold of the body, said: "It is very sad; but," he added, casting a look upward, "it is, after all, well that something hangs so high that it cannot be reached by every one."

BLAKKEN.[1]

BJÖRGAN was in former times the parsonage of the parish of Kvikne, in the Dovrechain. It was situated far up the mountain, quite by itself. As a little boy, I often stood on the table in the family sitting-room, and gazing down into the valley, watched with wistful eyes those who in winter skimmed along the river on skates, or in summer sported on the green. Björgan lay so high that grain would not grow there, and therefore the gard was sold to a Swiss traveler, and a parsonage purchased in the valley, where the conditions are certainly somewhat better. The coming of winter at Björgan was sorrowfully early! A field, which father had sowed by way of experiment one warm, early spring, lay one morning covered with snow; the mown hay was in quite as great danger from a snow-storm as from a heavy fall of rain; and when winter overtook us the cold

[1] The name usually given to a dun-colored horse.

was so great that I dared not take hold of the latch of the street door, lest my fingers should freeze fast to the iron. My father, who was born in that part of the country, near Randsfjord, and was thus well hardened to the climate, was, nevertheless, often compelled to wear a mask over his face when he drove to the distant sub-parish. The road creaked and groaned when one person came walking along, and beneath the footsteps of several it gave forth a sharp, shrill sound. Snow often lay on a level with the second story of the large building, while the smaller outhouses were entirely buried in it; hills, shrubbery, and fences were smoothed away, a sea of snow was spread around, with the tops of the tall birch-trees floating on its smooth surface, or it was lashed into billowy undulations by a storm which had here made hollows, there drifts. I stood on the table and saw the swift runners on snow-shoes faring away from us, down toward the valley. I saw the Lapps come whizzing down the mountains from the Röraas forest, with their reindeers, and up the slope toward us. Their pulkhas swayed to and fro, in the swift flight; and I shall never forget the moment when the party would finally draw up in our farm-yard, and a ball of fur would creep out of each pulkha and would prove to be a busy, cheery, little mortal, who sold reindeer meat.

The Kvikne dalesmen of latter days have developed into an enlightened, clever people; but at that time the Kvikne charge stood in worse repute than any other in the country. At not so very remote a date, a priest of that locality was obliged to carry pistols with him to church; another returned home from his churchward trip and found all his furniture cut to pieces and destroyed, by men whose faces had been blackened, and who had almost frightened the life out of his wife, who was at home alone. The last priest had fled from the parish, and had positively refused to return. The charge had been without a pastor for many years, when father — perhaps just for that reason — was called to it, for he was considered capable of keeping a boat still against wind and storm.

I still remember distinctly how, one Saturday morning, I was in the act of creeping up-stairs to the study, on hands and feet, because there was a coating of ice on the steps after the scrubbing, and had not proceeded very far when a crash and din from the study drove me down again in terror. For one of the champions of the parish had undertaken up there to teach the refractory priest the ways of the people, and had found to his dismay that the priest was resolved to teach him first his own. He made his exit from the door in such a manner that he came tumbling all the way down to the bottom of the stairs, and then gathering up his limbs, he reached the street door in four bounds. The people of Kvikne knew no better than to suppose that the priest gave them the laws that came from the Storthing. They wanted to forbid him to carry out the school laws; so, putting my father to defiance, they assembled in great force at the meeting of the school board, in order to hinder its actions with violence. In spite of mother's earnest prayers, father had repaired thither, and as no one else had ventured to aid him with the apportionment of the school districts, etc., he did it himself, according to his best judgment, amidst the thundering menaces of the crowd; but when, with the register under his arm, he went out from the assembly, they all gave way, and not a finger was laid on him. My mother's rejoicing can readily be imagined when she saw him driving home as calm as ever.

Under such circumstances and surroundings Blakken was born! His mother was a large red mare from Gudbrandsdale, the delight of every one who saw her; his sire was a madcap of a black fjord horse, who, one fine day, in a strange locality through which they were carelessly passing with the mare, burst whinnying out of the forest, and bounding over fences and ditches, came and took what was his own by the right of love. Of Blakken it was early said: "This will become the strongest horse that has ever been seen here in the North;" and accustomed as I was to stories about champions and fights, I looked on the little foal as a very highly-gifted comrade. He was, however, not always good to me. I still bear a scar over the right eye, the work of his hoof; nevertheless, I devoted myself with unwavering fidelity to both mare and foal, slept with them in the fields, and rolled between the mare's legs when the foal was feeding. But once I went too far with them. The day was warm; I had fallen asleep inside of a woodland barn whose door stood invitingly open, and where we had doubtless all sought shade; the mare and the foal had wandered farther, but I remained lying there. It was late in the day when those who had been calling and searching for me in vain came home with the tidings that I was nowhere to be found. The reader can imagine the alarm of my parents; every one joined in the search, went shouting through field and wood, carefully examined hills and precipices; until at last a child was heard crying in a barn, and I was found sitting on the hay. I was so frightened that I could not speak; for a black animal had been standing looking at me with eyes of fire. Whether I had dreamed this or actually experienced it, it would not be easy to say; certain it is, though, that even a few years ago I once awoke with this animal standing over me.

Blakken and I soon had playfellows: first a little dog that taught me to steal sugar, then a cat that one day made its appearance in the kitchen. I had never seen a cat before, and, pale as a corpse, I rushed into the sitting-room, screaming that a large mouse had come up from the cellar! The next spring our numbers were still further increased by the addition of a little pig; and then as often as Blakken accompanied his mother when she went about her work, the dog, the cat, the pig, and I came trooping after. We managed to kill time pretty successfully, especially by taking naps together. Indeed, I shared with these playfellows everything I liked myself: thus I once carried a silver spoon out to the pig, in order that it might eat nicer; and it tried, too, that is to say, to eat the silver spoon. When I accompanied my parents down to the valley to see people, the dog, the cat, and the pig went along. The first two were taken into the ferry-boat that was to carry us across the river, the pig, with a little grunt, then swam after us. We were treated to refreshments, each to suit his taste, and in the evening we went home again in the same manner.

But soon it was my fate to lose these comrades and retain only Blakken; for my father was called to the parish Næsset in Romsdal. It was a memorable day when we set forth, we children and a nurse-maid stowed away in a little house, secured firmly on a long sledge, that neither wind nor snow might assail us, and my father and mother in a double sleigh in front of us, surrounded by a group of people who wanted to say farewell over and over again. I cannot say that I was especially sorrowful; for I was only six years old, and I knew that at Trondhjem there was to be bought for me a hat and coat and trousers that I was to put on when we got to our journey's end! And there, in our new home, I was to see the sea for the first time! And then, too, Blakken was with us.

Here at the Næsset parsonage, one of the finest gards in the country, lying broad-breasted between two arms of the fjord, with green mountains above and cataracts and gards on the opposite shore, with undulating fields and eager life in the heart of the valley, and out along the fjord mountains, from which naze after naze, with a large gard on each, project out into the water, — here at the Næsset parsonage, where I could stand of evenings and watch the play of the sun over mountain and fjord until I wept as if I had done something wrong; and where on my snow-shoes, down in some valley or other, I could suddenly pause, as one spell-bound by a beauty, a yearning, which I was powerless to explain, but which was so great that I felt the most exalted joy as well as the most oppressive sense of imprisonment and grief; here at the Næsset parsonage my impressions grew, and one of the liveliest of these was that made on me by Blakken; for here he, also, grew. He became a hero, and did heroic work.

He was not very tall, but was extremely long in proportion to his height, and of a breadth that called forth an involuntary smile in the beholder; he was of a dun hue, rather inclined to the yellow than the white, with a black, extraordinarily full mane; he became a heavy, good-natured beast — in his every-day work, always hanging his head. His accustomed duties he performed as calmly as an ox, but most effectually. In addition to accomplishing more than half the horse-labor of the farming, wood-hauling, etc., on this very inconvenient gard, he did more than half the labor of hauling materials for a large, new main house and for the many additional buildings my father erected besides, and hauled it from a far-distant, awful forest. Where two horses could not pull the load, Blakken was used, and if the harness held he would bring it through. He liked to look over his shoulder at the boys while they piled on his double and triple load; of course he had not much to say about it, but he had to be told to go three or four times before he would heed the order, and even, then, he always first made a few trial pulls, — and then he started. He took his time, step by step. Sometimes there came a new servant who wanted to practice him in a swifter pace, but it always ended by the boy's learning the horse's gait. The lash was never used; for the powerful laborer soon became so dearly beloved that he was managed entirely by caresses. As Blakken gradually became renowned in the parishes, it came to be an honor, indeed, to drive him.

For Blakken was soon beyond compare the

greatest wonder of the diocese. It began, as is always the case when anything great starts up, with terrible uproar and hatred; it began, namely, by Blakken, who went out in the forest and on the mountain among the other horses of the parish, insisting on claiming all the mares for himself. He so severely bruised and gashed his rival suitors, who fancied that they could compete with him, that the peasants came rushing down to the parsonage with solemn imprecations and demands for damages. They thought it best, however, to have patience, when they saw that they would be vindicated under all circumstances; for Blakken's offspring did him honor! Still, it was for a long time a source of annoyance that his superiority was so immense and indisputable. Our neighbor, the lieutenant, could not, as a soldier, submit to this; he secured two heavily-built Gudbrands-dale horses, splendid animals, — and they were to teach Blakken respect. There were many wagers laid for and against; and how excited we were about the issue of the first encounter in the spring, up in the mountain-pasture! I shall, therefore, never forget the beautiful Whitsun evening when, as I stood out of doors listening to the black-grouse that were frolicking on the slope, a girl came running up and announced that both of the lieutenant's horses were standing close by the grindstone, near at hand, pressed up against each other. All hastened to the spot; and lo! the two superb animals stood trembling there, with blood streaming from wound after wound, — they had been under Blakken's monstrous hoofs and teeth! Terror had endowed them with strength to leap over the high picket fence of the parsonage; for they had not dared to pause before they had reached the house. The next day Blakken's praise was sounded along the church wall and was borne from there over mountain and strand.

Blakken had the sorrow of having one of his own sons, a spirited brown horse, share his sway with him for some years. He caught him in the midst of his first revolt, and as this audacious son would not take flight, but sent forth a challenging war-cry, the tried champion raised himself; they approached each other on their hind legs, threw their fore legs round each other's necks and wrestled. (Stallions always fight in this way.) Soon the young madcap described the arc of a violin bow; shortly after he lay crushed on the ground, and received his paternal chastisement. This I myself witnessed.

Almost every summer there were bears in the woods that killed many cows and sheep both for us and others. We were constantly startled by hearing the herd-boys halloo and the shepherd dogs bay; then the bells would ring, and the working people hasten to assemble and start for the woods with guns, axes, and iron bars; but as a rule their coming would be too late: either the dog would already have driven away the bear, or else the cattle had been stricken down ere help arrived. The horses could better defend themselves; but it happened now and then that the bear killed a horse, either by luring him into a swamp, where the horse sank and became an easy victim, or by getting him started on a race, so that he would plunge over a cliff.

One summer things were especially bad; there was scarcely a week that the bear did not attack our cattle; the horses would suddenly make their appearance close by the cattle pen, in a state of frantic alarm; for every time they had been chased by the bear. But Blakken, with the mare and the foal, which he with his sharp shoes held guard over, never came. We were in despair at last to know what had happened to them; the herd-boys had not heard the mare's bell for many days. As there had been a long-continued storm, during which the horses are apt to seek shelter near home, indeed often to station themselves just outside of the inclosure leading to the stable, and still they had not come, the boys were sent up into the woods in strong force in quest of them. They searched chiefly about the marshy lands, to see whether the bear might not have enticed thither the combat-loving horse, and thus overcome him and afterwards perhaps have taken both the foal and the mare, which naturally would have defended the foal. They sought and sought without detecting anything suspicious; the bear's footsteps (tracks as they are called) were everywhere to be seen, but no sign of any fight with a horse. As the boys walked on talking of this, and approached one of the finest grazing-grounds in the whole forest, one of them observed that just in the vicinity of a swamp there were tracks of the foal and the mare, but that they had been going round and round without stopping in the same circle, consequently in great alarm, and that this had happened recently, probably that same day. Upon examining the marsh they found truly enough that it had been torn up by the feet in a great fight. The boys began to feel hot and cold in turn, but they were determined to examine into the matter more thoroughly. On the brink of the swamp they saw traces of the hind feed both of bear and horse; they must then have both drawn themselves up at once, while the bear walked backward out in the swamp, in order to mislead the horse, and the latter followed; for the swamp can easily uphold the broad paw and calf of the bear; because he is not as heavy as the horse, who quickly sinks in and is caught there. But this time the bear had miscalculated; for although Blakken had sunk in pretty badly, the gigantic strength of his loins had sufficed to raise his legs from the mire of the swamp, while the sharp-shod forefeet beat, and the sharp teeth tore, and soon there could be found no further traces of the bear's hind-feet, but, on the other hand, an exact impression of his furry hide, and this was repeated over and over again through the whole swamp. He had been thrown down, had not been able to pick himself up again, but had turned over, and rolled round and round, in order to protect himself from the blows and bites of the infuriated horse, and this could be traced all the way to firm land. Inflamed by the exciting story of the battle-field, the hearing of the boys became sharpened, their sight more keen, and now in the still atmosphere, all glittering with sunbeams after the rainy weather, they could hear the mare's bell from the leafy wood at the foot of the ridge. They hastened thither, but were met by Blakken who with flashing eyes forbade them to come nearer. He was scarcely to be recognized. With head thrown back and floating mane, he was trotting round the mare and the foal in a large circle, and it was only after much kind talk and with the aid of salt, which they carried with them, that they could get him to recognize that these were friends who had come.

Now this, Blakken's great achievement, which was unique of its kind, threw such a halo about the animal's name that from being known as "the priest's Blakken," he was promoted to the title "Bear Blakken." Time upon time, year after year, he had his wrestles with the bear, and each time was long uncontrollable. He once came home bearing marks of the bear's claws; the fight had been with an old warrior who had seized the horse below the eyes, and had made terrible gashes there when Blakken had torn his head loose. To have such a fierce old stallion going sharp-shod about the woods and pastures was extremely dangerous; but the horses knew him and fled at his approach, and even if now and then one would be stupid enough to allow himself to get a thrashing, people were inclined to be forbearing with Blakken, on account of his great fame. A horse who could throw the bear to the ground might be allowed to do pretty much as he pleased.

How greatly admired he was could best be seen when we were obliged, as seldom happened, to employ him as a church horse. If the whole family with the governess and tutor wanted to drive to church, he had to draw three or four of us in an old gig, in which one sat "not merely for pleasure." As none of the ordinary harnesses were large enough for him, he had to hobble along in his working gear, and as his heavy bristling mane fell over his eyes, he did not look exactly suitable for a trip to church. He had to be put in the rear of the party; for in the first place he would not trot, but would only take the gait suitable for a working cart, and, in the second place, he wanted to carry the church-going people into all the woodland paths he was accustomed to tread. But if he went in the rear, he did to a certain extent as the others did; when the other horses trotted, Blakken plunged forward, and so those who sat in the gig were borne onward at a hobbling jerking pace, or as in a heavy sea, and on one occasion were actually made sea-sick. At church, on the other hand, there was an entire change. There were a great many other horses there, and throwing back his head he would send forth a veritable war-whoop. It would be answered from the fields round about, and off he would start with the gig, but would be held back, unharnessed, and tethered. He had his own special tether along, and was always tied in a place close to the foot of the mountain, in order to be as far as possible from the other horses. But if he wanted to join them, he would tug at his tether and raise himself on his hind legs, and send a long whinny down the slope. A larger number of people gathered about him than were seated in church; when he had been quiet a while, they would pat him, measure his breast, his neck, his hips, would take him by the mouth, in order to examine his jaws; but as soon as one of the other horses neighed, he would tear himself away from his admirers, start up and reply; this seemed to all beholders the noblest sight they had ever seen. I for my part have certainly never since been so proud of anything as I was in those days of Blakken, when I stood among the peasants, and listened to their loud resounding words of praise.

And here, at the summit of his triumphal career, let me leave him. I went forth into the world and found other goals for my admiration and other heroes to follow.

FIDELITY.

YONDER on the plains in my native parish, there dwelt a husband and wife with their six sons. They toiled faithfully on a very large but hitherto neglected gard, until an accidental wound from an axe ended the husband's days, and the wife was left alone with the hard work and the six children. She did not lose her courage, but led her eldest two sons forward to the side of the coffin, and made them promise her over their father's corpse to care for their little brothers and sisters, and to be a help to her as far as God gave them strength. They promised, and they kept their word until the youngest son was confirmed. Then they considered themselves released from their pledge; the eldest married the widow of a gardman, and the next to the eldest shortly afterward married her well-to-do sister.

The four brothers who remained at home were to have the entire management, after having until now been continually under control themselves. They did not feel much ambition for this; from childhood up they had been accustomed to keep together, either in couples or all four, and did so more than ever now that they must depend solely on one another for help. Not one of them would state his own opinion about anything until he felt sure of that of the others; indeed they were not certain of their own opinions until they had looked into one another's faces. Without having made any compact, there was still a mute agreement among them, that they would never separate as long as their mother lived.

She herself, however, preferred to have things somewhat differently arranged, and got the two who had already left home to agree with her. The gard had become a well-tilled piece of land; more help was needed, and so the mother proposed to pay the eldest two for their portion, and divide the gard among the four sons at home, in such a way that they would keep together in couples, each couple occupying half of the gard. There should be erected a new set of houses alongside of the old ones; two of the sons should take possession of them; the other two should remain with her. But of the couple that left home, one must marry; for they would need help about the house and the cattle; and the mother named the girl whom she would like to have for a daughter-in-law.

None of them had any objections to offer, but now the question arose, which two should move away, and of these two, which one should marry? The eldest of the four said that he was quite willing to leave home, but he would never marry; and each of the others in turn objected.

Finally they agreed with the mother that the girl should be allowed to decide the matter. And up at the summer stable one evening the mother asked her if she would be willing to come to the plains as a wife, and the girl proved to be quite willing. Well, then, which of the boys would she like to marry; for she could have whichever one she pleased. Why, she had not considered the matter. Then she must do so now, for it was left to her to decide. Well, then, she supposed it might be the eldest; but him, she was told, she could not have; he was not willing. Then the girl named the youngest. But the mother thought there would be something strange in that; "for he was the youngest."

"Then the next to the youngest!"

"Why not the next to the eldest?"

"To be sure, why not the next to the eldest?" replied the girl; for he was the one she had been thinking of the whole time, therefore had not dared name him.

Now the mother had judged, from the moment the eldest had refused, that this must be because he thought the next to the eldest and the girl had an eye on each other. So the next to the eldest married the girl, and the eldest moved with him into the new home. How the gard was now divided no outsider could learn, for the brothers worked together as they had done before, and they stored away their harvest, now in one barn, now in the other.

After a time the mother's health began to fail; she needed rest, consequently, help, and the sons agreed to engage permanently a girl who was in the habit of working here. The youngest brother was to ask the girl the next day they were gathering leaves; he knew her best. Now the youngest must for some time have had a secret liking for this girl; for when he came to speak to her he did it in such a singular manner that she thought he was asking her to marry him, and she said, "Yes." The youth was frightened, and going at once to his brothers told them what a mistake had been made. They all four became very grave, and none of them dared utter the first word. But the next to the youngest could see that the youngest really cared for the girl, and that was the reason why he was so frightened. At the same time he saw clearly that it was his own lot to be a bachelor; for if the youngest should marry he could not. This seemed to him rather hard, for there was one of whom he himself had thought; but now nothing could come of that. It was *he*, then, who made the first remark, namely, that they would be surest of the girl if she should come to the gard as the wife of one of them. Always when one had spoken the others agreed, and the brothers now went to talk with their mother. But when they got home they found their mother ill in earnest; they must wait until she was well; and as she did not become well again, they once more held counsel together. In it the youngest proposed that as long as the mother lay in bed no change must be made, and this was agreed to; for the girl must have no more to care for than the mother. Thus it remained.

For sixteen years the mother lay in bed. For sixteen years the intended daughter-in-law waited on her patiently and without a murmur. For sixteen years the sons met every evening for devotions at her bedside, and on Sundays the eldest two also joined them. She often begged them in these peaceful hours to remember her who had tended her; they understood what she meant by this, and promised. During all these sixteen years she blessed her illness, because it had allowed her to taste a mother's joy to the last; she thanked them every time they gathered about her bedside, — and one day this was for the last time.

When she was dead her six sons met to bear her themselves to the grave. It was customary here for women as well as men to attend funerals, and this time the whole parish followed, men and women, all who were able to walk, even the children; — first the deacon, as leader of the singing, then the six sons with the coffin, and then a long train of people, all singing so that they were heard more than a mile away. And when the body was laid to rest, and the six sons had filled the grave, the whole procession repaired to the church, for there the youngest son was to be married; the brothers would have it so, because this funeral and wedding really belonged together. Here the priest, who was my now deceased father, spoke so eloquently of fidelity that I, who chanced to be present, thought when I came out of church that it was something that belonged with the mountains and the sea and the grandeur of the entire surrounding nature.

A PROBLEM OF LIFE.

"WHY shall we sit down here?"

"Because it is high and light."

"But there is an awful precipice here; it makes me giddy, and the sun glares on the water. Let us go farther!"

"No; no farther."

"Then let us go back to the green glen; it was so beautiful there."

"Oh, no; not there either," and he sank down as though he could not or would not keep up longer.

She remained standing, with her eyes fixed intently on him.

Finally he said, "Aasta, you must now explain to me why you were so afraid of the foreign skipper who came in at twilight."

"Was not that what I thought," she whispered, and acted as though she wanted to run away.

"You must tell me this before you go, else I will not follow you."

"Botolf!" she exclaimed, and turned round, but did not stir from the spot.

"It is true, I have promised you not to ask," said he. "I will keep my word, too, if you prefer to have it so; but in that case it is all over between us."

Now she burst into tears, and walked right up in front of him. Her delicate little figure, her soft, light hair, from which the kerchief had fallen back, and then her eyes and mouth, — each strikingly individual and yet combined now in one expression; the sun was shining full upon her. He sprang to his feet.

"Ah, you know very well when you look thus at me, I always yield. But I have now also learned that it is only worse afterward. Cannot you understand this: if I promise you a hundred times not to want to know your past, I can have no peace. I cannot endure it!"

His face, too, bore traces of a suffering that did not date from yesterday.

"Botolf, that was just what you promised me, at the time when you would never let me have peace, you promised me to let it all rest, all that I could never, never tell you. You promised me this solemnly; you said that it made no difference to you; that it was only me you wanted! Botolf!" — and she sank down on her knees in the heather in front of him; she wept as though her life were in peril; she gazed at him, while tear after tear continued to speak for her, and she was the most beautiful and most unhappy being he had ever in his life beheld.

"God have mercy on me," said he, as he rose, but sat down again at once; "if you loved me enough to place confidence in me, how happy we two might be together!"

"And if you could only have a little confidence in me," she besought, drawing nearer to him on her knees, and then she continued: "Love you? That night when I came up on deck, after our ship had run against yours, you stood by the shrouds, giving orders. I had never seen anything so strong. I loved you at once! And when you carried me over into the boat while the ship was sinking, I felt a desire for life again, and that I had thought I never more should feel."

She ceased speaking, and she wept; but presently she clasped her hands on his knee. "Botolf!" she implored, "be great; be magnanimous, as you were that time when you took me, without anything else, — only me! — Botolf!"

Almost harshly, he replied, "Why do you tempt me? You know very well I cannot! It is the soul we want; it is not this. In the first days it is all very well, but not afterwards!"

She drew back, and said, hopelessly, "Oh, no! A life can never become whole again. Oh, my God!" Then she burst into tears.

"Give me your whole life, and not merely a fragment of it! and then it shall become whole again in my keeping!" He spoke with emphasis, as though to put courage into her; she made no reply, but he saw that she was undergoing a struggle. "Conquer yourself! Have courage! Worse than it is now, it cannot possibly be!"

"You can drive me to the worst!" she wailed. He misunderstood her, and continued: "Even if it proved to be the greatest crime, I shall try to bear it; but this I cannot bear."

"No, nor I either!" she cried, and rose.

"I will help you!" he rose too, as he spoke; "every single day I will help you, if I but know what it is. But I am too proud to be the keeper of something I do not know—and which may perhaps belong to another!"

Here she grew flaming red. "For shame!" she cried. "Of us two, I am the prouder. I do not offer what belongs to another Now you may cease!"

"Ah, if you are proud, take away my suspicion!"

"Good Lord, I can endure this no longer!"

"No, I have sworn that *this day* shall bring the *end!*"

"Is it not merciless," she cried, "to be willing to torment and torture a woman who has trusted herself to you, and who has prayed to be spared, as fervently as I have!" and her tears began to flow again, but with a sudden revulsion of feeling she burst out: "I understand you; you want to force that which is within me to cry aloud, so that you may thus learn something."

She looked at him resentfully and turned away. Then she heard slowly, word for word:

"Will you, or will you not?"

She stretched forth her hand. "Not if you were to offer me all that now lies spread before our eyes!"

She walked from him, her bosom heaving, her eyes restlessly wandering about, but chiefly seeking his face with an expression that was now hard, now agonized, now hard again. She leaned against a tree and wept, then she ceased weeping, but walked on as before.

"I knew very well that you did not love me," she heard, and in a moment was the humblest and most repentant of women.

She made several efforts to reply, but instead flung herself down on the heather and buried her face in her hands. He walked up to her and stood over her. She felt him standing there, she waited for him to speak, she covered her face, but as no words came, she grew still more frightened and had to look up. As she did so she sprang to her feet; his weather-beaten long face had become hollow, his deep eyes that were without eyebrows, his wide mouth, with its tightly compressed lips, his whole large, imposing figure, became impressed with such a concentrated, extraordinary force upon her that she suddenly saw him standing up by the shrouds, as on the night of the shipwreck. He had become as grand as he was then, and possessed of a boundless strength, but this strength was now turned against herself!

"You have lied to me, Aasta!" She retreated, but he came after her. "You have also made a liar of me; *there has not been perfect truth between us one single day of the time we have lived together!*"

He stood so near her that she could feel his warm breath; he looked right into her eyes until she grew dizzy; she did not know what she should say or do the next moment, and so she closed her eyes. She stood as though either about to fall down or to run away — the crisis was at hand. In the profound silence that preceded it, he himself grew alarmed. Once more he assailed her: —

"Give me proof! Lay aside all your arts; do it now, here!"

"Yes!" replied she, but without being conscious that she spoke.

"Do it now, here!" I say.

He gave a shriek; for at this moment, she dashed past him and over the brink of the steep; he saw her fair hair, her upward stretched hands, a kerchief that floated up, got loose, and fluttering after her was soon wafted far away. He heard no scream, nor a yet splash, for the depth was very great. Nor did he *listen;* for he had fallen to the ground.

From the sea she had come to him that night, in the sea she had disappeared, and with her the history of her life. Into the black night of the deep had plunged all that his soul possessed — should he not follow? He had come hither with the firm determination to put an end to his torment; this was no end, the end could now never come, this was only the real beginning. Her last act shouted up to him that he had judged falsely and murdered her! Notwithstanding this the agony had increased tenfold; he must live in order to ponder on how it had come to pass. She, who was almost the only one who was saved that terrible night, she had been rescued only to be murdered by him who had rescued her. He who had sailed about and traded as though the whole world was only a sea and a place of business, had suddenly become the victim of a love which had destroyed both him and the object of his affections. Was he wicked? He had never heard this said, and never felt it. But what was it, then? He rose — not to fling himself over the precipice, but to go down the mountain again; he would not put an end to his life the moment he had found a problem to solve.

But it could never be solved. She had lived in America ever since she was grown up; she was coming from there when the ship struck. Where in America should he begin? Where she was from in Norway he did not definitely know; he was not even sure that her surname was the one her family had borne in Norway. The foreign skipper? Ah, where was he? And did he know her, or was it only she who knew him? He might as well ask the sea; to journey away and begin an investigation was the same thing as to plunge into it.

He had been in error! One who was guilty and repentant would have eased her mind by confessing all to her husband; one who was not repentant would have sought to evade his inquiries. But she revealed nothing, nor did she seek evasion; she took refuge in death when pressed too sorely. Such courage did not belong to one who was guilty. Ah, why not? Rather death than confession; for still greater courage was needed for the latter. But she did not lack the nerve for confession; for she had certainly begun by confessing that there was something she could not tell him. It must be a crime that forbade it. But she could not have been guilty of any great crime; for she had often been happy, indeed merry; she was passionate, but she had fine feelings and was kind-hearted. The crime must be that of another. Why, then, not say that it was that of another; for in such a case his distrust would have vanished. But if it were neither hers nor that of another, what was it, then? She herself had certainly said that there was something — and then the foreign skipper of whom she was so much afraid? What was it, what in the name of wonder could it be? Had she still lived, he would still have continued to torment her — this thought stung him and made him wretched.

And his agonies did not cease. Perhaps she was not so guilty as she thought herself, or perhaps not so guilty as she must seem to others. How often is there not innocence behind our guilt, simplicity in sin, although so few can understand it — and *him* she had not believed capable of understanding it, because he was in a continual state of suspicion. Out of one straightforward answer he would have found occasion for a thousand suspicious questions, and therefore she had preferred to trust herself to death than to him! Why, had he never, never been able to leave her in peace? To *him* she had fled from her past, of *him* she had sought protection from it, and yet it was he who was constantly conjuring it up, and who continually let it loose upon her! She was truly devoted to him, she was affectionate and charming when with him — what then was her past to him? And if it did concern him, why had he not thought of it at first? No, according as her tenderness increased, his restlessness grew; the moment she became his, not only from admiration and gratitude, but from the heart, then he wanted to know if she had ever belonged to any one else, and what her previous life had been.

And the more it grieved her, the more she begged for mercy, the more he insisted, for he felt sure there must be something!

For the first time the thought occurred to him: had *he* told *her* everything? Was it really imperative to tell each other everything? Would all be understood as it really was? Most assuredly not.

He heard two children playing near him, and looked round. He sat in the green glen she had recently spoken of, but he was not aware of it until now. Five hours had rolled by, he thought it was but a few minutes. The children must have been playing here for some time, but he had not heard them until now. Ah! was not that Agnes, the priest's six or eight years old daughter? whom Aasta had loved to idolatry, and who was so much like her — God in Heaven; how like her she was! The child had just helped her little brother up on a stone, he was to play being in school, and she was to be the school-master.

"Now say what I say," said she. "Our Father!"

"Ou' Fath'!"

"Who art in heaven!"

"Heaven!"

"Hallowed be thy name."

"Ha'o'ed ey name."

"Thy kingdom come."

"No!"

"Thy will be done."

"No, I will not."

Botolf had stolen away walking backward; it was not the prayer which affected him, he had not even perceived at first that it was a prayer, but while he listened to and watched the children he suddenly appeared in his own eyes like a foul beast of prey, thrust out from fellowship with God and with man. Behind the bushes he retreated, that the children might not discover his presence; he was more afraid of them than he had ever been of anything in his whole life. He stole into the forest, far from the highway. Whither should he go? To the empty house he had bought and made ready for her? Or farther away? It mattered not; for wherever he could imagine himself, there she stood before him.

It is said of dying people that they have mirrored in their eyes the last thing they have seen; and he who awakens from an evil deed carries with him the first object his eyes rest on and never more becomes free from it. It was not Aasta he saw, as he had seen her lately on the heights; it was a little innocent girl—it was

Agnes. Even the image of Aasta as she sank from his sight became transformed into that of the child, with its small, uplifted hands. The remembrance of Aasta's unspeakable love for the child caused the images within his soul to undergo a mysterious change, the strong likeness played into the doubt of long months as to whether Aasta was guilty or innocent. Had Aasta just such a child nature concealed within her own breast? Yes, he had seen this, or rather, he knew now for the first time that he had seen it. Until now he had merely brooded over whether hers was the expression of innocence, whether she could have smiled thus to more than one, or in what way it was she had veiled this child she bore within her heart since it only had power to burst forth in radiant moments. A continual variableness in her nature, a restlessness with perpetual exaggeration, which also led others to exaggeration, had in her life both attracted and repelled him; now after her sorrowful death, all remembrances were centred in an innocent child engaged in prayer.

Where thought was piteously searching for light, he met the child; this barred every avenue to investigation. Every scene in their short life together, from that night of shipwreck until the Sunday morning on the heights —whenever he would question it, the child's face appeared, and this singular confusion of the two so wearied him in body and mind that after the lapse of a few days he was scarcely able to take any food, and ere long he was unable to leave his bed.

Every one saw that this was tending toward death. He who himself is the bearer of a problem, acquires a peculiar presence which makes him a problem to others. From the day he took possession here, *his* gloomy silence, *her* beauty and the hidden life of both created much gossip in the parish; when the wife suddenly disappeared the excitement grew until the most incredible things were the most readily believed. No one could furnish any information, inasmuch as none of those who lived or were occupied along the sea-shore or the mountain ridges, had had a view of the heights that Sunday morning just at the moment when she had flung herself over the precipice in the sunshine. Nor did her body drift ashore to bear witness itself. There were therefore stories afloat about him, even during his lifetime. He presented an ugly appearance, as he lay there in his bed, with his long, hollow face, which was surrounded by an unbroken framework of red beard and bristling red hair. The large eyes looked up as from a shut-in lake. As he seemed neither to want to live nor to die, it was said that there was a struggle about him between God and the devil. Some had even seen the evil one, surrounded by flames of fire, reach up to the windows of his chamber in order to call him. They had seen him sniffing around the house in the form of a black dog, or bounding in front of it like a rolling ball of wool. People who were rowing past had seen the whole gard on fire, others had heard a procession shouting, barking, laughing aloud, coming out of the sea, faring slowly toward the house, passing in through closed doors, rushing madly through all the rooms, and then with the same screaming, baying of dogs and neighing of horses, sweeping down to the sea again and there disappearing.

The servants of the sick man, men and women, left at once, and they told about all these things. No one dared go near the gard. Had not an old houseman and his wife, to whom he had been kind, now taken pity on him, he would have been left without any help. The old woman who waited on him was herself in great fear; she burned straw under his bed, in order to drive away the evil one; but although the sick man was nearly destroyed by fire, released he was not. He lay there in terrible suffering. The old woman thought finally that there must be some one for whom he was waiting. She asked him if a message should be sent for the priest. He shook his head. Was there any one else he would like to see? To this he made no reply. The next day, as he lay on his bed, he distinctly pronounced the name "Agnes." It surely did not come as an answer to her question of the preceding day; but the old woman took it for this. Delighted, she got up from her seat, and going out to her husband begged him make haste to harness the horse and drive over to the priest's for Agnes.

At the parsonage they thought there was surely a mistake, and that it was the priest who was wanted to minister to the sick; but the old man insisted upon it that it was Agnes. The little girl herself sat within listening, and was much afraid; for she also had heard about the devil and the procession from the sea; but she had also heard that the sick man was waiting to see some one before he could die, and did not think it was strange that it should be her whom his wife had so often carried home with her. The wishes of a dying person must be fulfilled, they told Agnes, and if she prayed like a good girl to her God, then no one could do her any harm. And she believed this, and permitted herself to be dressed for the visit.

It was a cold clear evening, with long attendant shadows, the sleigh-bells were echoed through the woods, it was somewhat alarming; but Agnes sat in the sleigh and prayed, her hands clasped inside of her muff. She did not see the devil, nor did she hear the procession from the sea, along whose strand she was driving; but she saw the stars above her, and the light on the heights in front of her. Up at the gard it was dismally still; but the old woman came out at once, carried her in, took off her travelling wraps, and bade her warm herself at the stove. And, meanwhile, the old woman said that she must be of good cheer and go bravely forward to the sick man and say the Lord's Prayer over him. When she was warm, the old woman took her by the hand and led her into the chamber. There he lay, with his long beard and his large and hollow eyes, staring at her. She did not think that he was ugly, and she was not afraid.

"Will you forgive me?" he whispered.

She knew that she ought to say Yes, and so she said Yes. Then he smiled and tried to raise himself, but was powerless to do so. She began at once with the Lord's Prayer, but he made a movement of protest, and pointed to his breast; and now she laid her two hands on it, for that was what she understood him to mean, and he laid his clammy, ice-cold, bony hand above her little warm hands and then closed his eyes. As he said nothing when she had finished, she did not venture to withdraw her hands, but began anew. When she had done this for the third time the old woman came in, looked at them and said,—

"You may stop, my child, for now he is released."